Peter Washington was educated at Manchester
Grammar School and Christ Church, Oxford,
where he wrote a thesis on the poetry of
Crabbe. Since 1976 he has organized and
taught on the Literature and Philosophy degree
at Middlesex Polytechnic, a unique joint ven-
ture in which critics and philosophers come
together to reflect on the relationship between
the two disciplines. His interest in interdiscipli-
nary studies, and his belief that criticism must
also be seen in the broader perspective, are also
reflected in his directorship of the Literature in
Context course at the English Speaking Union,
which places classic European texts of the eight-
eenth and nineteenth centuries in their cultural
setting.

Peter Washington has written on seven-
teenth-century tragedy and twentieth-century
fiction. He has recently completed a book on
theories of national character and is working
on a study of gurus. He is unmarried and lives
in London and Herefordshire.

FRAUD:
LITERARY THEORY AND
THE END OF ENGLISH

Peter Washington

FONTANA PRESS

First published by Fontana Press 1989
Copyright © Peter Washington 1989

Set in Linotron Sabon
Printed and bound in Great Britain by
William Collins Sons & Co. Ltd, Glasgow

Fontana Press is an imprint of Fontana Paperbacks, part of the
Collins Publishing Group, 8 Grafton Street, London SW1 3LA

FOR MY PARENTS

'Martin Finnucane,' I said, 'a hundred and two
difficult thoughts I have to think between this
and my destination and the sooner the better.'
Flann O'Brien, *The Third Policeman* (p. 49)

CONTENTS

Foreword

This is not another survey of recent literary theory but an attack on its institutional and political pretensions. I have therefore chosen to comment on a few representative, influential and accessible texts.

These pages owe a good deal to my discussions with staff and students in the Literature and Philosophy Division of Middlesex Polytechnic. My thanks are due to them, and especially to Doreen Maitre, Jeff Mason, Claude Pehrson, Jonathan Ree, and other members of the Staff Research Seminar who are responsible for the stimulus needed to write this book, but not for its contents. I am also grateful to Diana Avebury, Max Egremont, Roger Lubbock and Jamie Niedpath for the hospitality and encouragement they gave me while writing the book; to Helen Fraser for commissioning it; to John Bayley for commenting on an early draft; and to my editor Stuart Proffitt.

The seven chapters' epigraphs are all taken from that masterly critique of futile theory, Flann O'Brien's *The Third Policeman* (MacGibbon and Kee, 1967; respectively pages 33, 145, 171, 52, 50, 167 and 111).

1

The Problem

> This is very edifying, every sentence a
> sermon in itself. Ask him to explain.

What follows is a polemic directed against literary post-structuralist pretensions to disciplinary, cultural and political authority, and the strategic obscurity in which those pretensions are cloaked. This book is not an attack on literary theory or radical politics as such, but on the fruit of their irregular union: Radical Literary Theory (RLT for short). My particular target is the belief that varieties of this theory (and there are many), and more particularly their deployment inside the academy, are suitable vehicles for changing the world. I object to this not because of the political content of such theories (which must always be a matter for dispute) but because of their institutional context. Colleges are not the place for inculcating doctrines but for examining and criticizing them. They constitute our best public arena in which ideas can be tested without regard to particular interests. This has become a controversial view in our time, when the notion of disinterested debate is under fire from all sides; but I believe it still constitutes the best – and perhaps the only – defence of literary, philosophical and historical study at undergraduate level, and the proper justification for the academy's slight aloofness from the world. This aloofness is not a matter of disconnection from the conflicting interests in which all the participants are, like everyone else, inevitably involved, but a temporary suspension of those interests in favour of dispassionate understanding.

That one should have to argue this case may surprise many

readers, who have always assumed anyway that universities and polytechnics are, for better or worse, ivory towers, where some individuals spend a few years or even their whole lives cloistered from reality in the interests of learning; but recent years have seen increasing pressure on all aspects of academic life to become 'relevant'. From the right, this pressure usually takes the form of an insistence that all forms of education pay their way and prove that they are doing so. That is one way of winnowing the ideological wheat from the chaff. The left hopes to achieve similar results by different methods. It insists that teachers either demonstrate their commitment to radical reform, not only in their politics but also in the material they teach and the way in which they teach it; or that they admit their 'complicity' (a favourite word) with the repressive institutions of bourgeois society. The criterion on the right is utility, on the left rectitude. While I would be inclined to agree that the challenge from both sides has been salutary in waking the literary academy out of its slumbers, I believe that neither demand is, in the end, acceptable. This does not, however, commit me to what has become known as the liberal humanist, i.e., middle of the road, view that higher education in the humanities should be in the business of transmitting certain cultural and moral values connected with individualism, democracy, personal development and so on. My point is precisely that it is not our business as teachers to transmit values of any kind, whether right, left or centre, in an institutional form. Our business is to develop the mental capacities of our pupils. Which is why I have chosen in this book to attack the dogmatic tendencies of radical literary theory, and its insidious inclination to mask crude indoctrination in pseudo-technical jargon. As we shall see, there are good reasons why RLT comes largely from the far left. Had I the space, I would argue at equal length against the equally ideologically based right-wing passion for utility (which is, in its way, just as crude and just as manipulative) and against the liberal humanist view that literary education is a means of transmitting specific values. But at present, RLT represents the worst, because the subtlest and most insidious, threat to intellectual honesty in the literary academy – and, let us admit, the most interesting. If the intellectual fraud comes mainly from the left, so does the intellectual vigour. That makes its failings all the more dangerous.

It should be said at once that there is nothing new either in post-structuralist claims to authority or in the obscure jargon which often accompanies them. Both tendencies are present in literary theory from its earliest days in the attempts of Plato and his pupil Aristotle to answer certain questions relevant to their philosophies. What are poetry and rhetoric? How do they work? What effects do they have? What effects *should* they have?

In the course of formulating these questions, the two philosophers established ways of thinking about literature which are still current. Aristotle – the founder of literary criticism – largely confines himself to cataloguing rhetorical forms and their functions. He concentrates on formal properties, evolving a technical vocabulary which already illuminates the virtues and vices of theory. His attempt to generate a general theory of tragedy remains a model of genre criticism, its terminology sometimes illuminating, but frustratingly elusive. The way in which a term such as 'catharsis' tells us everything and nothing, for example, should alert us to the problems of advancing beyond the simplest theoretical discussion of literary texts.

We find a very different emphasis in Plato, who is altogether more interested in literature's social and moral role, and in the relationship between literary discourse and power – in other words, in literature's political status. Plato is sensitive to the poet's unmatched capacity for good or ill. While Aristotle is inclined to see poetry and rhetoric as means to an end, ways of communicating and persuading,

Plato has a vision of writers as dangerous men who can disturb the order of the state if they choose by inflaming the imaginations and emotions of the people. It is for this reason that he demands their subordination to political direction; and his theory of literature is devoted to discussions of the form and purpose of this direction.

Each philosopher's attitude to theory (and they are paradigmatic) is determined by his view of literature. For Aristotle, theory is a way of explaining literature. His theory of tragedy is not meant to govern the production of all future tragedies; it is an empirical account of what tragedy has been, based on existing texts. For Plato, however, theory is a way of mastering literature, just as philosophy is (among other things) a way of mastering politics. It has often been observed that Plato's own practice contradicts his principle. He is a great poet whose rhetorical effects escape the control of his logic. But this only reinforces his point about the subversive power of poetry, and the state's need to control it.

Plato's literary theory is, of course, not only parallel to his philosophy, but also a part of it. In the ideal scheme outlined in *The Republic*, poetry is not merely to be censored: it is itself a vital instrument of social control. Poets are governed in order to govern the people, who are not merely to be protected from evil but positively instructed in the ways of good. Poetry – and the theory which controls it – are not objects of knowledge, as in Aristotle, but weapons in a political war.

The contrast between Aristotelian detachment and Platonic engagement has never appeared to be more relevant than it is now, and nowhere more so than in the literary academy, where a complex row rages about the place of theory in the curriculum, and the role of literary education in the modern state. The rhetoric of institutional politics often presents this row in simplified form: old versus new, theorists versus critics, tradition versus reform; but there is a sense in which it transcends all these oppositions, taking us to the heart of

insoluble questions about the nature of existence, the relationship between literature and reality, and the place of culture in
education. Given the range of possible views on these topics,
it might be said that the row is not, as many believe, a
distraction from the proper business of the literary academy,
but constitutive of it: even when the arguments are about the
very grounds on which the debate is to be conducted, their
rehearsal itself forms the basis of an education. Academic
discourse is concerned less with finding answers than with
formulating and discussing questions. It teaches us not what
to know but how to think. In this sense, the theoretical
challenge has been fruitful.

Yet there is another sense in which the very opposite is true
– the sense in which ideologists of right, left and centre reject
the 'how to think' argument in favour of positive indoctrination, however muted. In this sense, the debate has not been a
rational examination of disagreements, but a partisan squabble about rights and wrongs. Ironically, this squabble is in
part the product of the literary academy's very success over
the last century. A hundred years ago, departments of vernacular literature did not exist: now they take a lion's share of
the academic cake. But the usual price of imperial expansion
has been paid, in terms of exposing internal weaknesses and
the crossing of that invisible line between the confident self-
scrutiny so necessary in the life of any complex institution,
and the neurotic self-questioning which spells its doom. The
debate about the uses of literary education has now come
perilously close to a weary feeling that the question is not
only unanswerable but hardly worth asking.

One major reason for this development is the idiotic
polarization of Platonists and Aristotelians – a polarization
which is seen by many of the participants in the row to focus
on the issue of theory, and which is actively encouraged by
them. One has to be either 'for' engagement or against it, for
theory or against it, for progress or against it, and so on. But
the rhetorical opposition I set up earlier between Plato and

15

Aristotle is misleading. The problem is not that academics choose one stance or the other, but that they tend to opt for a dangerous mixture of both. On the whole, intellectuals incline to Aristotelian methods and Platonic ambitions. They cultivate system and classification, the daily grind of arranging knowledge in order, but they hanker after stronger meat. This is especially true of literary intellectuals. Perhaps Plato is right: their feelings are stirred by the inflammatory material they deal with. Or perhaps it is just self-evidently true that the prospect of ruling the state is more intoxicating than the prospect of merely ruling the classroom. This is the prospect Plato offers, and it has proved especially enticing to his recent heirs on the far left. Forced out of mainstream politics by circumstance (and often by choice) and exasperated by the baffling strength of the Western liberal democracies, they have been forced into a campaign of guerrilla war against all kinds of bourgeois authority (except their own), even when it takes the comically limp-wristed form of academic literary criticism, portrayed as an especially vicious agent of repressive capitalism. But being intellectuals and academics, they are driven to couch their campaign in suitably dignified – i.e., Aristotelian – language. The result is Radical Literary Theory.

This is a crude simplification – but not, I believe, a distortion of the situation. Nevertheless, uninvolved readers may still wonder why and how radical theorists choose such a vehicle. Surely direct political action of the terrorist kind would be more effective than composing obscure treatises – especially when these works are Aristotelian to the point of an obscurity which surely makes them self-defeating? There are two answers to this question, a simple one and a subtle one.

The simple answer derives once again from Plato. If literature is as powerful as he claims, and theory therefore so important, it follows that control of literary education is one key to political power. Radical theorists who see schools and colleges as central instruments of state power naturally want to take them over.

But why do they do this in such an arcane fashion? Here comes the subtle answer. Plato and Aristotle based their theories on a concept of representation which sees art as a copy or imitation of the world. The critic's business is either (in Aristotle's view) to comment on the accuracy and force of the imitation or (in Plato's view) to dictate its political content. But since their time the theory of representation as imitation has been replaced by the idea Wilde summed up in a famous phrase when he suggested that Nature imitates Art, and not the other way round, i.e., that representations do not conform to our prior knowledge of reality, but are instrumental in providing us with that knowledge. We apprehend the world through our representations of it.

This version of Kantianism confers a peculiar authority on artists, the most distinguished makers of representations in our culture. It also makes the poet a paradigm of characteristically human activity, in the sense that we each make the world through the representations socially given to us. But it also confers considerable authority on those who can explain this process – theorists. Furthermore, in its extreme form, the doctrine implies that reality is not merely given to us: we can alter it by changing our representations. Hence, for example, the feminist idea, that we can change the status of women by reinterpreting the ways in which they have been represented in literature.

Once again, this is a crude summary, but it sheds some light on the radical notion of textual politics. The theorist's business, according to this notion, is not to explain critical theories but to change the world. In order to do this he must create a language untainted by old-fashioned notions of representation. Theoretical texts thus become a means of mastering our perception of literary texts, which in turn shape our apprehension of the world. The theorist is thus constituted as a Platonic governor by means of an Aristotelian language.

We shall see how this works in practice in some of the

following chapters, where I shall suggest that among the major schools of radical theoretical thought, structuralism and deconstruction have an Aristotelian bias, whereas Marxism and feminism are the province of all-out Platonists – the characteristic radical literary theory being a judicious blend of the two strands, accommodating the passion and revolutionary objectives of Marxism and feminism with the vocabulary of structuralism and deconstruction. For now, however, I want to return to my opening remarks about the importance of disinterest in literary studies and its relevance to the present state of the academy.

The examples of Plato and Aristotle are once again relevant. The symbolic battle between them has been fought out many times and on many different grounds, but at no time more dramatically and symbolically than in the Renaissance. That the complexities of that movement are quite beyond the scope of the present study is unimportant compared with the strength of its self-images which are still vivid today – in particular, the self-image of humanist scholars who presented themselves as challenging a derelict status quo, much as RLTs do now. Then, as now, the issue at stake was ideological, i.e., political, and the academy was only one part of the battleground, but within it the reformers marched under the banner of Plato, who stood for enlightened reason and free enquiry. The enemy was the Aristotle of medieval schoolmen: a rulebound pedant who valued tradition over truth and institutional orthodoxy over individual heresy. In Renaissance iconography, Plato invariably appears as a pagan saint, Aristotle as a dull pedagogue.

At stake in this conflict was the question of ultimate authority: the conscience versus the church, the individual versus the state, the scholar versus the institution, and so on; and one could draw many parallels between humanist scholars and RLTs – which would be ironic because it is precisely the humanist inheritance RLTs say they are trying so hard to displace (though, as we shall see, they are mistaken in this

hemselves necessarily civilizing. It hardly needs Steiner-
portraits of camp commandants relaxing with Goethe
a heavy day at the ovens to bring to mind something
ing us in the face with every television news bulletin. Yet
ical theorists, who contemptuously dismiss the humaniz-
g power of liberal education, and the social benefits of
dvanced technology, are still prepared to believe in the
edeeming power of textual politics.

They are not alone. Trust in cultural institutions has largely
replaced belief in religious and moral sanctions among the
European and American intelligentsia, who still cling to the
hope that universities and publishers can succeed where
churches fail. This is linked with the fetishizing of 'creativity'
as our era's supreme value – with an irony which hardly
needs underlining. Who is not familiar with media gurus
solemnly apostrophizing imagination, creativity and spon-
taneity with all the divine fire of depressed funeral directors?
The more cumbersome and pervasive the cultural machine
becomes, the more its discredited priests hanker after the lost
paradise it seems to represent. But somewhere among all the
ritzy programmes about painters and the learned articles
about writers and the symposia about composers, something
is getting lost. 'Culture' is becoming a ghastly burden, another
ideological dead-weight, like the medieval church and modern
communism: intended as a means of salvation and turning
into its own opposite. The absurd earnestness of theory,
signalled by its verbal redundancy, is not only part of this
burden, but its most serious symptom. And its frantic search
for new languages and a pure realm of its own, where it can
relax untainted by the bourgeois horrors of reference and
experience, suggests that even the gods of culture are now
becoming discredited and need replacing, as they once seemed
about to replace the gods of religion.

It is hardly surprising that the pain of all this is felt most
acutely in college literature departments where teachers daily
confront the chasm between their growing cultural burden

view). But once again, the opposition between Platonists and
Aristotelians is more rhetorical than real. Not only were
many humanist scholars at least as bigoted and narrow as
their opponents, as the religious wars of the seventeenth
century testify, but even the symbolism is misleading. For the
real hero of liberal humanism at its best is not, of course,
Plato, but his master Socrates. The dogmatic philosopher-
king of *The Republic* far outdoes Aristotle in cultural author-
itarianism; and compared with Socrates, both Plato and
Aristotle look peremptory. Both are concerned to exert their
hegemony in the name of Reason, i.e., philosophy.

The situation is much the same among the minor Platos
and Aristotles of the contemporary academy, where the
question of authority is once again at stake. Like every
academic discipline, literary studies can be validated in a
number of ways: (1) by reference to a body of agreed rules;
(2) by direction from a higher authority (such as the state);
(3) in relation to an external standard (such as reason, utility,
philosophy or theory); or (4) by appeal to tradition, in the
form of conventionally established practices and objectives.
Methods 2 and 3 look similar enough to be identified in
practice, as are methods 1 and 4. One might say that the first
pair are Platonic, the second Aristotelian. But for most of the
time the academy muddles along on a mixture of all four,
with some practitioners inclining to one, some to another. It
is only in times of crisis (except insofar as academic life is
permanently in crisis) that the differences become important,
as they have now.

This has happened because the academy has become the
focus of a power struggle between factions on the left and right
and in the centre. The legitimate claim that education is a
political issue has been subtly manipulated by all sides into the
view that it is a party-political issue – a matter of taking sides
and laying down ideological principles. It is asserted, most
vociferously by the left, that one cannot avoid doing this in any
domain of life, least of all in pedagogy, where the content takes

precedence over and determines the form. We are exhorted either to take up the radical cause, or to defend the academy from its dangers. But taking sides is surely only one part of politics, unavoidable though it may sometimes be? There is a preliminary move – namely, knowing why we should take one side rather than the other. To believe that all knowledge is irretrievably conditioned by interests – that we can never finally stand a little apart from any situation and decide on its merits – is to make party politics irrational and therefore pointless, and the academy itself an irrelevance. If the only purpose of education is to reinforce our prejudices, there is not much use in it. We can do this in far easier and cheaper ways.

My argument in this book is a simple one: that it is precisely *because* knowledge is largely conditioned by interests, and because our existence is irretrievably political, i.e., subject to conflicting demands and powers, that the cultivation of detachment, rational enquiry and scepticism (in the general sense) are absolutely essential; and why they remain the foundation of the academy in general and the literary academy in particular. We must have domains, however limited, unsatisfactory and even compromised, in which reflection is possible. That is the view outlined in this book, first through a discussion of how we arrived at the current situation, then through a critique of some major radical theoretical positions, and finally by reference to some tentative ideas of my own.

The problem with an identity crisis is that any authority appealed to for validation turns out to require a higher authority itself. This is compounded by the fact that loss of faith cannot be remedied by rational argument, only by the discovery of another faith which needs no authority other than its own to validate it. So once a task becomes not merely a task but a matter of acquiring fundamental beliefs, the individual charged with the task is in trouble. Imagine a

plumber who had to refer all his
metaphysical critique every time he
changed a tap. His job would becon
He could never find sufficient grounds
activities: these are only supplied by th
necessity. The contemporary academic
physically disposed plumber: he is cons
grounds other than practice for validation
while knowing throughout that those grou
provide the validation he seeks. There is, in s
mate' reason for literary study apart from any
the individual may possess.

It may be that this has always been the case
problems we encounter even in Plato and Aristotle
inability to supply any but arbitrary grounds for
study. But it becomes far worse when literary st
constituted as an academic discipline. When that hap
problems of purpose and methodology become not incide
but essential. For this reason we cannot altogether bla
RLTs from taking up the riddle of a sphinx who has becon
steadily more impatient since the second half of the nineteenth
century, when vernacular literature began to appear on the
syllabus in a major way. They are only repeating lessons
learnt from their predecessors. In particular, they have before
them the example of critics from Arnold and Sainte-Beuve to
Leavis and Lukács, all of whom make the loftiest claims for
the study of vernacular literature as a self-sufficient domain
and the basis of humane learning. RLT is no different in this
respect from the lofty waffle which passes for criticism, and
there's little to choose between Arnoldian tosh about the
uplifting qualities of great poetry, and Althusserian tosh
about the uplifting qualities of ideological demystification.
Arnold thinks culture should try to save the world, Althusser
prefers to call on 'science'. Both are deluded.

Literature cannot save us. In our own century we have
painfully relearnt this lesson: that civilization's products are

and the ignorance and even hostility of their students. The pain is none the less for being part of the professional apparatus: the wry, self-deprecating manner of tutors embarrassed by having to foist all these boring old books on to their pupils. What price Leavisite claims to the cultural hegemony of literary studies when one is reduced to wheedling the occasional ill-written essay out of a resentful tutee whose understanding of how commas function – let alone critical theories – is uncertain?

The irony here is that as the level of student competence and cultural knowledge declines, theory becomes ever more sophisticated and arcane, and teachers find themselves increasingly isolated in a curious twilight zone between the two. No wonder an identity crisis sets in. Ironically, this crisis is an effect of the cultural and educational boom of our own century – the boom which produced so many literature teachers in the first place. The enormous increase in literacy (and here standards have risen, not fallen), made possible by increasing prosperity, has stimulated the massive expansion of higher education in the humanities; but the beneficiaries of this development, i.e., the mass of undergraduates, have not been able to keep pace with the intellectual complexity of their subject which is growing at an exponential rate. First academic criticism, and now theory, have developed a momentum of their own, urged on by the growing number of critics and theorists whose task it is to write articles and books about one another (like the present volume) and whose jobs depend increasingly on the volume of their publications. The result of this momentum is more and more specialization (usually called professionalism) and a galloping intellectual elitism. In consequence, the realms of literary theory and literary pedagogy grow further and further apart.

Although reflected to some extent in the world outside, this is a peculiarly academic dilemma. Literary papers and periodicals are ruled by the laws of the market. In the end, critics writing for a public must make themselves understood and must address their readers' concerns if they are to survive. But the literary academy is a closed, self-validating institution, whose funds are dependent not on pleasing an audience but on academic success – which is defined in the terms laid down by literary academics. There is therefore also a growing split between academic and public criticism, as the first turns more and more in on itself, and is more and more subject to the power of theory.

Such a tendency is equally disastrous for teachers and pupils, for criticism and theory, for the academy and the state. The consequences for criticism are clear enough to anyone who peeps into an academic journal. What should be instrumental and economical – a teaching model for students and a means of communication – is too often a self-serving Frankenstein's monster with a will of its own. And so far has this process gone, that 'instrumental' is itself a dirty word among some radical theorists who reject absolutely the idea that literary criticism's main function is the illumination of primary texts. The traditional view is that we read Eagleton to understand, say, Shakespeare, not Eagleton. In some remarkable cases – Johnson, Coleridge, Lukács – the critic may be more interesting than the texts he discusses, but this is not normally the case. Nor do odd examples invalidate the view that what matters about the literature/criticism distinction is not essential but functional: we go to some texts to help us out with others. To deny this and to constitute criticism (and/or theory – the distinction between them is often blurred) as an autonomous realm is part of the radical argument which wants to make criticism/theory not a means to understanding the world, but a means of changing it.

One consequence of this view is the inversion of a traditional order of precedence which makes theory serve criticism, and criticism serve literature – or, more accurately, readers of literature. According to RLT, criticism is subordinate to theory – and so are readers, in the sense that their

24

responses can be determined, modified or predicted by sufficiently comprehensive (though as yet unformulated) theoretical accounts of what literature and reading are. Once again, we are back with Plato, in whose republic the citizens will be formed by the guardians of the state. This is not so much a case of saving the world as of making it in the theorist's image.

Theory has always had its place in the academic study of literature, even at its most empirical. At the very least it is necessary as a corrective to such study's innate tendency to lapse into aimless historical, generic or thematic scholarship on the one hand, or the mere taxonomy of taste on the other. What Barthes calls science (i.e., theory), criticism (scholarly commentary) and reading (the expression of aesthetic preferences) have always been legitimate activities. It is the relationship between them which has changed according to circumstances, both inside the academy and without. The eternal quest is to find some way of accommodating all three in a coherent framework.

This is made more difficult by the fact that, as anyone even slightly acquainted with the nightmare world of American learning will know, the current theoretical war is as much an institutional power struggle as an intellectual campaign: it is about who gets what academic jobs. Such battles are endemic in institutional life and ultimately incidental to it. What makes this one *appear* to be far more important is that radical theorists take it to be a major battle in which there is something far more significant at stake than their own welfare: nothing less than the cultural and political control of society.

In my view this belief is wildly out of line. The passage of time in RLT's brief career (thirty years at the most) is already revealing it as a continuation by other means of what it most dislikes, i.e., traditional literary criticism. Very little RLT is even theory in the strong sense, i.e., a body of abstract, invariant general principles. Most of it is simply an elaborated form of conventional academic practice with a *soupçon* of ill-absorbed philosophical jargon. And the irony is, that the more successful radical theorists are in storming the bastions of the bourgeois academy, the more they resemble their opponents, staunch pillars of the institution. Traditional critics who fear theory often tremble for the wrong reasons. If they are ousted by their opponents it will be because they have been outclassed in orthodoxy.

There is nothing new here. Academic life is a history of fashion wars and that is just as it should be. It is the business of intellectuals to test new ideas – the trouble begins when they are seduced by the first handsome theory in their path. Instead of a brief flirtation, they indulge in a heavy affair, with the usual disastrous consequences. There is no reason to suppose that semiology and grammatology will last any longer than anthroposociology or theosophy, or any of the other -ologies and -osophies do. But the art of the academic game is to be a ruthless lover and not become trapped with one girl or another.

Needless to say, this is not how the matter looks to most radical theorists (except perhaps Barthes) for whom constancy is at a premium, at least until the current theory has been superseded. They regard the love-her-and-leave-her approach with due moral solemnity as politically irresponsible, culturally dishonest and academically suspect. Such butterfly behaviour is, in their view, just what has been wrong with literary studies since their inception as a university subject almost a century ago. It is precisely, they believe, such unprincipled dilettantism which has now brought the whole discipline to its present sorry state – a state which it is part of their brief to remedy. They propose to do this by injecting ever more theory until literary studies look suspiciously like a disguised form of philosophy. But this will only be an appearance, for the ultimate aim is to replace philosophy's anyway discredited claims to be the foundation of humane learning with their own. Literary theory is, in short, to become the queen of the human sciences, and is to occupy the throne occupied in their time by philosophy and theology. It is no accident that the theoretical campaign is never more bitter than when attacking Arnold, Leavis and their continental counterparts. These men also aimed to put literature and criticism at the top of the disciplinary hierarchy. The theorists are their children – and whom does the rebellious child resent more than the father he so closely resembles?

Twenty years ago in the seedy aftermath of the 1968 *événements*, these ambitions looked briefly, if remotely, plausible to the enthusiastic few. Now they are little more than an embarrassing memory, and radical theorists are left with the problem of what to do with a project which was meant to change the world and now has difficulty changing itself, so close is it to lapsing into the very bad habits it was meant to cure: a topic for the taxonomy of popular guides (Fourteen Ways of Looking at a Text) or the basis of incoherent rhapsodies on the coming socialist millennium (Every Person Their Own Paradigm, or One Text for All and All for One).

It is partly as a consequence of this failure that the struggle within the academy has now become so fraught, as theorists, balked of larger prey, turn their attention to their own backyard. But as the crisis of confidence spreads to theory itself, what was once presented (by radicals) as a conflict between thrusting theory and entrenched bourgeois criticism (no doubt smoking a large cigar and trampling the faces of the workers) can now be seen as a half-hearted tussle between two equally tired parties. The demoralization this implies on all sides is probably worse than all-out battle, and the issue at stake now is not how literary studies should be governed, but whether we should bother with them at all. Is there really a place for them in the modern academy? Can we justify the large numbers of undergraduates reading vernacular literature? And if not, what should we be doing about it?

My preoccupation in this book is radical theory's role in

this debate – and in particular, the spuriousness of its political claims.

These claims are ultimately founded on a simple and simply misleading rhetorical opposition between RLT and bourgeois, i.e., conventional, academic criticism. The opposition is factitious because there is no such entity as bourgeois criticism, which is a straw man set up by radical theorists to give substance to their own project. Leaving aside for the moment the fact that the word 'bourgeois' has been made almost meaningless by abuse, we can certainly agree that there are bourgeois critics – if by that we mean unreflecting supporters of an unexamined intellectual and political status quo (though it is difficult to think of any famous examples); but it takes hardly any historical knowledge at all to know that, of all intellectual pursuits, literary criticism, even in its most subdued periods, is the most characteristically combative (unless, of course, we intend to relegate everything written before 1968 to the bourgeois realm, in which case there is no argument).

What is true of bourgeois criticism is equally true of RLT, which is distinguished by the ferocity of its internal battles. The difference between the two is that radical theory is given an *apparent* unity of purpose by its opposition to bourgeois criticism – precisely the reason for inventing that myth, of course: without it, the incoherence of radical theory would be even more apparent than it is, and the motley crew of Marxists, feminists and deconstructors shown up for the minor pressure groups they are.

There are two significant ways of dividing up the four theoretical brands that I consider in this book. First, one can think of them either as ideological campaigns (Marxism and feminism) or as methodological techniques (structuralism and deconstruction). But one can also make a rather different division in terms of those (structuralists and Marxists) who believe in the possibility of a theoretical science, i.e., a discourse providing general, abstract and invariant interpretive principles; and those (feminists and deconstructors) who, by denying such a possibility, paradoxically constitute themselves as theorizing anti-theorists.

Add to all this the fact that these divisions are not watertight, and that examples of all these approaches can be found under any of these headings – so that one can have, for example, feminist theory, feminist anti-theory, politicized feminism, a-political feminism, a-political theoretical feminism etc. – and the confusion is clear enough. Add to *that* the glee with which all four schools plunder every intellectual discipline from linguistics to anthropology (in ways which make radical complaints about bourgeois criticism's amateurism look ludicrous) and the stage is set for chaos.

Now this chaos would hardly matter – on the contrary, it could well be regarded as a creative profusion – were it not for the present tendency among radical theorists to attempt a major synthesis of elements from all four schools (not to speak of psychoanalysis, reception theory, formalism etc.); the synthesis which goes under the name of post-structuralism, documented in many recent books, and which is said to be, in some fundamental sense, a new and improved way of looking at the world. This is a vague way of putting a vague claim of the sort previously made for unfortunate precedents such as rosicrucianism and theosophy, both of which strike me as very appropriate comparisons because they, too, were founded on undemonstrable assertions about the ultimate destiny of Man (or should one say Person?). No harm in making such assertions, of course, no harm at all. On the contrary: there is a sense in which the more extreme theory is, the more it adds to the gaiety of nations. Doubts exist about tone and manner – the tone of a thousand articles and text-books which now debate these ideas as though the argument were about matters of detail, when in fact the whole theoretical edifice is built on air.

Take, for example, the central doctrine of radical critical theory which contrasts, as usual, two dominant models, radical and bourgeois. The bourgeois critical ideal is said (by

RLT) to be a matter of articulating common thematic pre-occupations in a common language. The bourgeois critic treats texts as though they were messages from writer to reader: his job is to explicate the message rather as a window-cleaner wipes the glass, clearing away obscurities and facilitating immediate contact between reader and text – a text which is, in turn, a direct expression of the writer's intention. This view is said to depend on certain assumptions: that reader and writer are both autonomous subjects with identifiable intentions; that these intentions can be communicated; and that literature is capable of representing them, either directly or symbolically.

Catherine Belsey, summing up this complex of ideas as expressive realism,[1] suggests that behind this critical model there lurk all sorts of improbable beliefs concerning the nature of intersubjectivity and the referential properties of language. Ultimately it rests on an implicit theory of human nature which ignores the political/cultural context of every speaker, and the fact that all propositions, critical and otherwise, are determined by the limits of our language. Her argument is unconvincing, whether or not one agrees with her account of human nature, because it is impossible to find a major bourgeois critic who states the doctrines she attributes to them or implicitly abides by them. Even the most sternly rational eighteenth-century commentators – Boileau, Pope, Johnson – concede the non-referential qualities of literary language, the uncertainty of interpretation, and the peculiar status of fiction; while the twentieth-century realists she seems to have directly in view – Lukács and Leavis – concede that what a writer 'expresses' may not be what he 'intends'.

Having disposed of the bourgeois model, Belsey – being herself a Leavisite believer in the moral and political value of literary criticism – then sets up a radical critical practice replacing the bourgeois trio of author/book/reader with her own sequence of writer/text/decoder. Authorial intention gives way to ideological inscription and the critic turns from mediation to production. The text is no longer a representational message, but a fragment of the general textuality within which the critic may intervene. There is no structural difference between the two models: in both the critic interprets texts in relation to contexts (reality, textuality, history, intention etc.). But there is said by RLT to be a crucial functional difference. Bourgeois criticism is mediational and objective, radical criticism strategic and engaged. Or rather – both forms of criticism are said by RLT to be strategic and engaged: the real difference is that radical criticism admits this while bourgeois criticism does not. Bourgeois criticism's claims to objectivity in fact mask its surreptitious support for the political status quo (assuming that is not already radical itself, of course). The bourgeois critic elects to reproduce passively (and often unconsciously) the (deplorable) values of bourgeois society, while the radical critic elects to challenge them, in the process becoming a textual guerrilla at the social margin (assuming comfortable academic jobs count as such a margin). In the Sartrean scheme of things which, for all the current unpopularity of its vocabulary, still underpins most radical thought, the critic must choose freedom or involve himself in a paradox. He is either for freedom or against it – in which case, his activities as an intellectual contradict the very nature of intellectual life, which is to evolve towards freedom.

Thus even the most fearsomely elaborate RLT is founded on a simple moral choice between subversion and complicity, and the traditions of thematic criticism are waved away as so much unenlightened debris. But the formula is not only crude: it is involved in its own paradoxes. First there is the bland historicism which assumes we know more today than we did yesterday: by next week this will render Belsey as irrelevant as all her predecessors. Then there is the difficulty of squaring RLT's egalitarian pretensions with its intellectual remoteness. A lot of ink has been spilt on this topic, with radical critics (including Belsey) wearily pointing out that clarity, lucidity and plain language are part of the bourgeois mythology by means of which the proletariat are kept in their place. This argument holds that bourgeois criticism's ideological strategy is to pretend that literature (and its attendant discourses) simply reflect (and thereby reinforce) a fixed order of reality, in which the bourgeois have firm control over the means of production (among which cultural discourses, such as theory and criticism, are major elements). And anyway, it is often added, theory and criticism have always had specialized jargons of their own, so what's the difference? Radical theorists thus manage to have it both ways, by accusing bourgeois critics of amateurism while enlisting that amateurism on their side.

This is part of Terry Eagleton's approach in *The Function of Criticism*, which accounts for the fraudulence of the bourgeois critical model by adducing Habermas's theory of the public sphere. Briefly, Eagleton's claim is that Western culture has created a myth of public literary discourse in which all subjects (i.e., individual participants) are deemed equal in their relationship to an ideal of rationality, though they are in fact included or excluded from such discourse by that very ideal which is a disguised form of bourgeois power. Objectivity, lucidity, common sense, etc. are ultimately expressive of specific political interests. The bourgeoisie define them, defining themselves and the limits of their power in the process.

There is, of course, no way of proving this and no way of disproving it. The relevant point is that it moves all forms of discussion about literature on to political grounds by means of claiming that they are already there anyway, and it is only a bourgeois mystification to pretend that they are not. Eagleton produces an ingenious history to make his point – but it would hardly be difficult to produce a counter-history to show the opposite. But perhaps the really significant thing about Eagleton's book is that, like Belsey's, it contradicts its own principles by cultivating in practice bourgeois ideals of rationality, lucidity and objectivity. Both writers claim to be describing the facts of the case, as opposed to other presentations of the same issues; and both writers do a good job of interpreting their intimidating sources – such a good job that it is relatively easy to unpick their arguments.

But in the end the issue of theoretical language is a red herring. Worrying about whether the proletariat are well served by Lacanian baroque is just another way of moving the argument on to radical theory's territory before it even begins. Forcing the opposition to speak your language is a well-known way of winning arguments. But if you deny the possibility of a common language, however qualified by specialist terms, you might as well give up arguing in the first place. If I speak Russian to pure anglophones, I might as well talk to myself – and this is precisely what much extreme radical theory does. It is thus caught between two stools: either it submits to 'translation' or it opts out of the larger debate altogether. Doing the first involves submitting to commonly agreed rules of discourse. Doing the second means abandoning the chance to make a wider impact. These two alternatives are the two poles about which RLT uneasily revolves: the desire to construct a convincingly politicized pedagogy and the urge to invent a private dialect in which theoretical desires frustrated in the world can be fulfilled, and even imposed on the critical community.

This last objective – the academy's conversion to theory – is often attempted under the name of scholarship and intellectual responsibility. Every real discipline, it is argued – and the physical sciences are one model here – has a theoretical corpus with its own language. Of course some of what biochemists do is ultimately popularized, but this is a last step: it would be quite intolerable to expect the practitioners of a science to operate with crude common sense and everyday language. Without the tools of their trade, progress would be impossible. Without a theoretical language it would be impossible to inscribe hypotheses. Indeed, it might be impossible for such a science to exist at all. A discipline is demarcated from other disciplines by the terms it uses and the special ways in which it defines them.

These are all persuasive arguments for theory and a distinctive theoretical language – but only if we accept the initial premise that academic criticism (as opposed to literary scholarship) is indeed a specialized discipline, and the province of a few experts. But the situation of literary studies has been complicated ever since their inception by the fact that this is not quite the case. Of all academic discourses, criticism is – and always has been – the one which hovers most uneasily at the door of the ivory tower, with two faces, one looking in, the other out. Of all discourses, it is the one which can least afford to lose its direct contact with the outside world – a point amply borne out by its fate when this happens. Literary studies do not really constitute a discipline at all. They have found a home in the academy under false pretences. And their proper role is not to rule the human sciences but to stimulate them: to act as a rogue element in the ever-mortifying academy. This is the only sense in which they are political, irrespective of party viewpoint.

I shall have more to say on this topic, but before considering remedies for some of the problems outlined above, we need to see what is wrong with the radical project, by examining its constituent elements.

In a book so much concerned with the politics of theory, it is natural to take interpretation as the central issue. Politics, after all, is about points of view, about ways of looking at the world. Hermeneutics – the science or art of interpretation – has always been at the heart of critical debate. There are two linked questions we can ask about it. How does it work? Should it – and can it – be controlled? We might say that the first is Aristotle's question, the second Plato's. The first is a matter of critique, the second of ideology. But critique and ideology are never far apart, especially in the work of the three thinkers who have most profoundly influenced RLT:

Marx, Nietzsche and Freud. Between them, these three have effectively destroyed the notion that interpretation could ever be finally grounded in rational explanation or objective reality. Or should one say that the interpretations placed on their work and synthesized into RLT have done this? For the idea of interpretation – that there is no accessible reality but only our representations of it – has become so pervasive, that it is hardly possible within post-structuralism to attribute this or that doctrine to this or that thinker. Add that all three of these exceptionally brilliant men are riddled with self-contradictions, and the way is open to hermeneutic infinity. Not for nothing are many recent books about A's reading of B's reading of C's reading of D etc.

What makes this rather surprising is that only a few years ago, structuralism's project (as opposed to post-structuralism's) was the abolition, or at least the control, of such interpretative profusion. Structuralist critical theory is foundational in the strict sense, i.e., it attempts to provide general, abstract, invariant rules governing all interpretations (not only of literary texts). These rules are to be codified as grammar and poetics, and thought of as a scientific theory of literature as distinct from criticism, which is concerned with specific interpretations. Such rules were intended to be applications of a larger science of Man – a key to universal knowledge, of the sort eighteenth- and nineteenth-century thinkers were inclined to dream about.

But this project, though highly influential, was short-lived – less than two decades. It was not long before academics discovered, in their usual fashion, what everyone else knew already, i.e., that such a universal knowledge is both impossible and uninteresting. Most unusually, this discovery was announced at a specific time on a particular day, by one man, when Jacques Derrida, the progenitor of deconstruction, proclaimed the end of structuralism in his paper 'Structure, Sign and Play in the Human Sciences'.[2] Derrida has since had more influence in the literary academy than any other single man, and his rise to fame and dominance has been spectacular. His work is complex, but he is an anti-foundationalist and a contextualist. He rejects the possibility of a general theory as metaphysical delusion, and replaces it with what Hirsch has called local hermeneutics, i.e., a theory of interpretation which refers not to principles but to contexts. He is thus a kind of anti-theoretical theorist, and deconstruction is a form of conceptual scepticism, whose objective is the questioning of all cognitive distinctions.

Although the majority of structuralists (there are still some about) and deconstructors are probably committed socialists or Marxists of one sort or another, there is, properly speaking, no necessary ideological connotation in either doctrine. They are critical methods, not political stances, the one claiming interpretive authority, the other celebrating hermeneutic variety. But ideology and critique, like terrible twins, are never far apart. In Paris, where they arrange these things, structuralism and Marxism are roughly contemporaneous as significant forces in radical theory, involved in a complex dialogue from Sartre to Barthes. Similarly, feminism emerged as a force at about the same time as deconstruction.

These couplings are significant. For while Marxism and structuralism both see themselves as sciences (though there is difficulty about the interpretation of that word), deconstruction and feminism reject the scientific project as deluded. The first two are foundational, the second two anti-foundational. The first two are theoretical, in the sense that they see the evolution of a coherent and comprehensive theory as the vital step in their projects. The second two are anti-theoretical, in the sense that they reject the authority of totalizing concepts.

This is all rather confusing (and it remains to be seen whether subsequent chapters will deepen or dispel the darkness), but it seems to boil down to two questions. First, Is a science of criticism possible, and if so, what would it look like? And second, How can criticism – scientific or otherwise – be put to appropriate political use in the radical cause, i.e., in the service of revolutionary change? Despite my extreme scepticism about the value of RLT, I believe these are important questions which must be discussed if literature, criticism and theory are to survive in the academy in any useful form – and for that reason I overcome a native distaste for a genre which often seems about as socially useful as train-spotting.

Before turning to the theory proper, however, it may be useful to survey its historical and institutional context, if only for light relief. Academic life is a comedy shot through with moments of tragedy and farce. For the most part, theory belongs with the farce.

2

Mythologies

> One passage described by Bassett as being 'a
> penetrating treatise on old age' is referred to
> by Henderson (biographer of Bassett) as 'a
> not unbeautiful description of lambing oper-
> ations on an unspecified farm'.

The theoretical farce has always been most engagingly played
in Paris, where a whole troupe of ermine-clad feminists,
Marxist uxoricides, and polymorphously perverse professors
stand ready to perform on any excuse. Cambridge, by contrast, offers only the most tepid footnotes to a text written in
French, and it is perhaps typical that *l'affaire* McCabe
produced little more than a yawn in a country where the
public is either less intellectual than in France, or more
sophisticated, according to one's viewpoint. Ominously for
the future of theory, however, there are signs that even the
French audience is wearying of one naughty *maître à penser*
after another baring his bottom in public, and that the age of
theoretical scandals is over. The whole business certainly has
a curiously dated air, belonging to the 1960s and 1970s,
together with pop festivals and self-consciously wild parties,
at which appearance counted for more than reality. Those
who grew up in that era may remember the feeling that
somehow everyone but them was having a good time and
knew what was going on – and theory is a bit like that, too.
All the participants are inclined to predict the imminent
arrival of a solution to all our theoretical problems – a
solution which will come from somewhere else; but it never
arrives. In the world of RLT everyone is 'out of it' because

38

view). But once again, the opposition between Platonists and Aristotelians is more rhetorical than real. Not only were many humanist scholars at least as bigoted and narrow as their opponents, as the religious wars of the seventeenth century testify, but even the symbolism is misleading. For the real hero of liberal humanism at its best is not, of course, Plato, but his master Socrates. The dogmatic philosopher-king of *The Republic* far outdoes Aristotle in cultural author-itarianism; and compared with Socrates, both Plato and Aristotle look peremptory. Both are concerned to exert their hegemony in the name of Reason, i.e., philosophy.

The situation is much the same among the minor Platos and Aristotles of the contemporary academy, where the question of authority is once again at stake. Like every academic discipline, literary studies can be validated in a number of ways: (1) by reference to a body of agreed rules; (2) by direction from a higher authority (such as the state); (3) in relation to an external standard (such as reason, utility, philosophy or theory); or (4) by appeal to tradition, in the form of conventionally established practices and objectives. Methods 2 and 3 look similar enough to be identified in practice, as are methods 1 and 4. One might say that the first pair are Platonic, the second Aristotelian. But for most of the time the academy muddles along on a mixture of all four, with some practitioners inclining to one, some to another. It is only in times of crisis (except insofar as academic life is permanently in crisis) that the differences become important, as they have now.

This has happened because the academy has become the focus of a power struggle between factions on the left and right and in the centre. The legitimate claim that education is a political issue has been subtly manipulated by all sides into the view that it is a party-political issue – a matter of taking sides and laying down ideological principles. It is asserted, most vociferously by the left, that one cannot avoid doing this in any domain of life, least of all in pedagogy, where the content takes precedence over and determines the form. We are exhorted either to take up the radical cause, or to defend the academy from its dangers. But taking sides is surely only one part of politics, unavoidable though it may sometimes be? There is a preliminary move – namely, knowing why we should take one side rather than the other. To believe that all knowledge is irretrievably conditioned by interests – that we can never finally stand a little apart from any situation and decide on its merits – is to make party politics irrational and therefore pointless, and the academy itself an irrelevance. If the only purpose of education is to reinforce our prejudices, there is not much use in it. We can do this in far easier and cheaper ways.

My argument in this book is a simple one: that it is precisely *because* knowledge is largely conditioned by interests, and because our existence is irretrievably political, i.e., subject to conflicting demands and powers, that the cultivation of detachment, rational enquiry and scepticism (in the general sense) are absolutely essential; and why they remain the foundation of the academy in general and the literary academy in particular. We must have domains, however limited, unsatisfactory and even compromised, in which reflection is possible. That is the view outlined in this book, first through a discussion of how we arrived at the current situation, then through a critique of some major radical theoretical positions, and finally by reference to some tentative ideas of my own.

The problem with an identity crisis is that any authority appealed to for validation turns out to require a higher authority itself. This is compounded by the fact that loss of faith cannot be remedied by rational argument, only by the discovery of another faith which needs no authority other than its own to validate it. So once a task becomes not merely a task but a matter of acquiring fundamental beliefs, the individual charged with the task is in trouble. Imagine a plumber who had to refer all his activities to a logical and metaphysical critique every time he fitted a lavatory basin or changed a tap. His job would become well-nigh impossible. He could never find sufficient grounds in metaphysics for his activities: these are only supplied by the immediate hygienic necessity. The contemporary academic critic is like a metaphysically disposed plumber: he is constantly referred to grounds other than practice for validation of his activities, while knowing throughout that those grounds can never provide the validation he seeks. There is, in short, no 'ultimate' reason for literary study apart from any private faith the individual may possess.

It may be that this has always been the case – that the problems we encounter even in Plato and Aristotle imply an inability to supply any but arbitrary grounds for literary study. But it becomes far worse when literary study is constituted as an academic discipline. When that happens, problems of purpose and methodology become not incidental but essential. For this reason we cannot altogether blame RLTs from taking up the riddle of a sphinx who has become steadily more impatient since the second half of the nineteenth century, when vernacular literature began to appear on the syllabus in a major way. They are only repeating lessons learnt from their predecessors. In particular, they have before them the example of critics from Arnold and Sainte-Beuve to Leavis and Lukács, all of whom make the loftiest claims for the study of vernacular literature as a self-sufficient domain and the basis of humane learning. RLT is no different in this respect from the lofty waffle which passes for criticism, and there's little to choose between Arnoldian tosh about the uplifting qualities of great poetry, and Althusserian tosh about the uplifting qualities of ideological demystification. Arnold thinks culture should try to save the world, Althusser prefers to call on 'science'. Both are deluded.

Literature cannot save us. In our own century we have painfully relearnt this lesson: that civilization's products are not themselves necessarily civilizing. It hardly needs Steiner-ian portraits of camp commandants relaxing with Goethe after a heavy day at the ovens to bring to mind something staring us in the face with every television news bulletin. Yet radical theorists, who contemptuously dismiss the humaniz-ing power of liberal education, and the social benefits of advanced technology, are still prepared to believe in the redeeming power of textual politics.

They are not alone. Trust in cultural institutions has largely replaced belief in religious and moral sanctions among the European and American intelligentsia, who still cling to the hope that universities and publishers can succeed where churches fail. This is linked with the fetishizing of 'creativity' as our era's supreme value – with an irony which hardly needs underlining. Who is not familiar with media gurus solemnly apostrophizing imagination, creativity and spon-taneity with all the divine fire of depressed funeral directors? The more cumbersome and pervasive the cultural machine becomes, the more its discredited priests hanker after the lost paradise it seems to represent. But somewhere among all the ritzy programmes about painters and the learned articles about writers and the symposia about composers, something is getting lost. 'Culture' is becoming a ghastly burden, another ideological dead-weight, like the medieval church and modern communism: intended as a means of salvation and turning into its own opposite. The absurd earnestness of theory, signalled by its verbal redundancy, is not only part of this burden, but its most serious symptom. And its frantic search for new languages and a pure realm of its own, where it can relax untainted by the bourgeois horrors of reference and experience, suggests that even the gods of culture are now becoming discredited and need replacing, as they once seemed about to replace the gods of religion.

It is hardly surprising that the pain of all this is felt most acutely in college literature departments where teachers daily confront the chasm between their growing cultural burden

Institutional Myths

As we have seen, RLT's main institutional myth is the founding opposition between itself and bourgeois criticism. But this rhetorical flourish contradicts the actual circumstances of the case: RLT is the continuation of bourgeois criticism, not its negation. There is therefore a disabling irony at the very root of the radical project, which is engaged on self-destruction from the outset.

To do them justice, many of those who have shaped recent theory – notably Barthes and Derrida – are well aware of this; and in consequence they make it the starting-point of their work. Barthes, for example, remarks that every radical doctrine becomes an orthodoxy sooner or later. The only options are permanent revolution – an endless flight from one's own last idea – or anarchism: an indifference to theoretical consistency. Barthes practised both with mercurial brilliance, but the end-result is a curious sense of *déjà vu*. Each of his texts expends enormous skill and labour to demonstrate truisms. When all is said and done, Barthes is the Red Queen of theory, running hard to stay in the same place.

The problem of recuperation – the accommodation of radical ideas in the bourgeois consensus – is a major theme in RLT. How is it possible to construct RLT's immensely elaborate framework without being compromised by the institutional structures (academic, conceptual and linguistic) that framework seems to require? Are not the very conditions necessary to theory's evolution fatal to its radicalism? Is there not an inertia in the bourgeois academy which ineluctably drags everything back into its orbit? Theory's jargon is meant to be one solution to these problems, on the grounds that new concepts need a new language. Concluding from the post-structuralist synthesis of Saussure and Wittgenstein that

41

we cannot think beyond the limits of our language and that the structure of language pre-empts the structure of thought, radical theorists nevertheless hope to make a breakthrough. They can sustain this hope because the apparent pessimism of Saussure and Wittgenstein can be set against the utopian Marxism which informs so much theory, and which hints at an era, after the withering away of the bourgeois state, when we will be released from the bonds of every kind of bourgeois discourse, not only political and economic but also sensuous and conceptual. RLT is an attempt to anticipate that era and to bring it forward. Its bizarre styles are a foretaste of the life to come.

For RLT has a strong millenarian streak in it. The zealotry with which many devotees pursue it is more than a little reminiscent of sixteenth-century Geneva. Rigour and vigilance are favourite words, assumed to be virtues irrespective of context. Theory is a route to salvation, not an optional extra like knitting or playing the oboe. Like strenuous exercise, it is good for you, and the taste for it divides the world into elect and reprobate. In short, RLT is a church, and theorists are not Erastians. Given half a chance, they will restore ecclesiastical dominance over the state.

This sounds melodramatic because it is. Radical theorists are no shyer about their utopian claims than they are about their own authority, which rests on those claims. This church requires priests, experts of the letter, trained in the minute analysis required to interpret their own arcane scriptures, and to mediate between them and the people. Expertise is always open to abuse by those who use it for their own ends. Theorists are no exception to this rule. In an age compelled to put too much faith in the specialist – whether of the body or the mind – we should beware of them.

And we should beware of them especially because they insist so much on their own authority, via a highly selective interpretation of the past. This takes the form of presenting the bourgeois academy as irretrievably amateur and shallowly optimistic. Read Eagleton or Belsey, for example, and you will conclude that, with the exception of Raymond Williams and one or two other lonely heroes, English studies have been in the grip of bluff, bland, dense, genial misogynists who don't believe what they can't see and can't see what they don't already believe: Gradgrinds and Bounderbys of the mind, untouched by the real intellectual traditions of continental Europe. Not to have read deeply in Nietzsche and Heidegger, Benjamin and Adorno is not simply to derive from a different tradition, with a different outlook, but to be cast into spiritual darkness and professional ineptitude. Perhaps the most extraordinary aspect of this attitude is, once again, the almost religious faith it betrays. Having sternly cast aside bourgeois prejudices, characterized as an unreflective trust in appearances (usually called empiricism for reasons difficult to fathom), theorists are ready to accept the saints of the alternative tradition on trust. This is an all-or-nothing policy. You might cavil about details in Freud – his misogyny, for example; or Heidegger – his Nazism – but that doesn't stop you swallowing the theory whole, because it goes with a whole lot of other theories which are now part of the recognized radical baggage.

This baggage includes too many items to enumerate here, but some of them are worth picking out. First, the belief that significant thought is always oppositional, counter to prevailing values. This offspring of dialectic only applies outside the radical domain, of course, and on its behalf. Being oppositional to RLT is not a healthy challenge, but bourgeois obscurantism. Being oppositional within it is encouraged at the saner end of theory, but not among shriller feminists (for example) who will not brook contradiction.

Also deriving from the Kant/Hegel/Marx inheritance on which RLT thrives is the notion that struggle is always and everywhere desirable, outside Utopia. This is really another way of talking about opposition, and it underpins not only the intellectual style of RLT but also – and more significantly

– its moral and political stance. RLT is part of the wider class struggle of proletariat against bourgeois, i.e., providing a role for the literary intelligentsia, otherwise relegated to the sidelines like old-fashioned women and children. Opposition and struggle are an excellent way of virilizing or Amazonizing theory and making it, above all, relevant.

They are also ways of identifying an heroic alternative tradition – part of RLT's historical mythology – together with another strand of thought from the German Idealist tradition, canonized for radical theory by Freud: that things are never what they seem but always something else. Everything is symptomatic, a text to be interpreted. Apart from conferring immense authority on those duly qualified to interpret – therapists, theorists – a simple shift in this idea makes it possible to rewrite reality at will by weakening or even cutting the link between referent and reference, cause and symptom, topic and text, reality and appearance. Starting from the valid and undeniable points that we have no ultimate objective knowledge or certain grasp of 'reality' and every reason to suppose we never will have, it is easy to move to the claim that we therefore have *no* knowledge or that we have knowledge *only* of appearances which are *therefore* our reality. These arguments pop up in a thousand infinitely more sophisticated forms but they add up to the same thing: a charter to disregard the traditional or conventional body of opinion on the grounds that its very traditions and opinions make it suspect, in favour of edited alternatives.

Finally, these doctrines taken together can be deployed to legitimate a central RLT practice: reading against the text, i.e., using what texts do not say or what they explicitly deny, to support interpretations conformable with radical prejudice. By this means the apparently conservative great writers of the canon – James and Conrad are favourites – can be used to demonstrate radical theory's truisms. This is a version of the claim that when a girl says No she means Yes – which makes its popularity with feminists all the more surprising;

44

and it is the most striking example of radical bad faith, to pervert the idea that people *sometimes* do not mean what they say to the theory that texts *never* do. More of this in due course. For now let us merely note the convenient way in which RLT's basic tenets need never contradict the evidence, which can always be adapted and absorbed to prove its case. As Popper and other critics have remarked à propos both Freudianism and Marxism, theories which cannot be disproved because they are infinitely adaptable are not worth much. This is not to deny that Freud and Marx (not to speak of Nietzsche, Heidegger and the other saints of RLT) give us powerful and often persuasive descriptions of reality: only that we should beware of erecting their insights into legislative systems. There is no more sense in limiting ourselves by the worship of Marx or Freud than by the cult of a naïve realism – especially when such worship is patently self-contradictory. If a text always means Yes when it says No, where does that leave us with RLT itself?

It leaves us, as a matter of fact, with a whole chain of ironies, among which the most profound is the irretrievable complicity of theory with the bourgeois academic institutions from which it takes its life. This is well symbolized – in appropriately radical fashion – by the comic disjunction between the lives of most theorists and their views: fierce fire-raisers and revolutionaries on paper, mild men and women with dogs and mortgages in life. One sign of this disjunction is the aggression with which they fight for jobs in the very institutions they despise. This is more evident in America than in Britain. Feminists, who covet the very power they despise, are often especially culpable. The ghost of Leavis still walks.

To be fair, the academy is a real problem for radical theorists. It seems that they cannot ignore it, they cannot live without it, and they cannot live with it. Yet paradoxically, their success – were takeover of the academy to constitute success – would also be the failure of their doctrines of struggle and opposition. In other words, they have to cultivate a stance of permanent rebellion, even when there is not much to rebel about (though that in itself is often a good enough cause for some). This can be rebellion against institutional power structures or against critical 'institutions', i.e., ways of thinking and writing, themselves. In some quarters of the radical camp, these amount to the same thing: the political organization of society largely determines the way we write and think and vice versa. The two are involved in a huge circle or spiral which only theory can break out of.

One way out of this circle would surely be to dismantle the system? This is part of the radical programme – except, apparently, insofar as it concerns the literary academy. Robert Scholes, a moderate theorist, puts the problem like this: 'We cannot replace the apparatus because we are implicated in it. We cannot shut it down because it sustains our professional lives.'[1] Such embarrassing frankness is rare but the sentiment is common. It is apparently reason enough to keep universities going that they pay their employees and sustain their sense of identity. But notice the use of 'professional' here and imagine a comparison with medicine or law (to cite model 'professions'). Would one decline to shut down hospitals or courts because they 'sustain our professional lives'? Hardly. These professions – whatever one may think of them – have a positive and definable use in the world in ways academic criticism and theory do not – and that is the problem. Apart from the discomfort for a few individuals, would it really make any difference if every literature department in the world were shut down? That is what the question about theory's institutional life really comes to: is it of any conceivable use? This is the real political question about theory and almost no one seems ready to face it.

Instead, radical theorists indulge in fantasies whose basis is a picture of the world in the image of the academy: a model of reality which has no application outside itself, except to play a role in the chain of metaphors which leads from the brute realities of existence (where there is no funding for the literary academy, for example) to a utopia in which the only activity is the exegesis of texts. Perhaps this is another sad example of academic life's notorious tendency to render its inmates institutionally dependent, by making the university into the universe, the Church Triumphant on earth.

In the short term, these illusions have been given credence by the huge expansion of higher education since the Second World War and the consequent increase in graduate and research programmes. The motives behind this expansion were admirable, the unintended consequences less so, among them the wearying proliferation of journals, conferences, research seminars and theses, many of which are patently unnecessary before they even begin. This proliferation was encouraged by the internal logic of the institution, especially in America, where publication is essential to promotion, and visibility the key to academic success.

Perhaps most research in any domain is necessarily redundant: it has to be gone through to eliminate possibilities, which is one way of making progress. But this redundancy is compounded in literary studies by their uncertain utility outside their own field, outlined above. The result is what looks suspiciously like academics endlessly taking in one another's washing. Dr Y replies to Professor X, in turn eliciting twenty responses from colleagues. The discussion continues until everyone is exhausted, when it moves on to another topic. This is the usual pattern of literary research. It has obvious pedagogic value, in the sense that the learning is in the argument itself, but does it really merit inscription in the paraphernalia of journals and conferences which characterize contemporary academic life? And are we not fooled by this paraphernalia into seeing more at stake than there actually is? Once again we must ask the question: would it make any difference if the whole machinery collapsed?

A good many publishers and others involved in service

industries would certainly say Yes. They have contributed a good deal to the rolling of academic waves over the years. It is, of course, in their interest to stimulate these waves, to ensure that as one intellectual fashion follows another, more and more explanatory texts are needed, and the well of production need never run dry. The paperback market is a vital element in modern Western education, and the two support one another. Every lecturer receives pre-publication notes, booklists and the promise of free inspection copies relevant to their courses, if they will only recommend the text in question to enough undergraduates. Perhaps this is a good thing, promoting the flow of ideas, but one does wonder. There is so much money at stake – and so much prestige – in both the academy and the publishing industry, that no one has time to stop and think. As Scholes rightly says, so many professional lives are in question – and who would dare to tamper with them?

Theory's fate in all this has been intriguing. Once the province of a few specialists, it has become a mushroom industry in the last two decades, in the academy and in academic publishing. The reasons for this are complex. Nor can they be explained purely in sociological terms. Nevertheless, Western society's prosperity and technological advance, and the educational and cultural expansion this has made possible, play important parts if only because they created the right conditions for a rapid acceleration in the literary academy's internal development – rather like putting too much manure on the garden.

Briefly, one might say that prosperity created a vacuum, in more senses than one. Offer a humble peasant the money to do anything he likes, and the result might be similar. Literary studies had muddled along for half a century in the old ways, giving their succession to Latin and Greek as a sufficient reason for existence, whether in the modest formulation of Raleigh and Quiller-Couch or the arrogant rhetoric of Leavis. Suddenly, this was not enough. Expanding resources arrived together with shrinking credibility. If postwar natural and social sciences were going to solve the problems of life then literature, philosophy and history were luxuries, albeit luxuries we could well afford. So the paradox of the last half-century is that these subjects were expanding as never before at the very moment when they were losing their *raison d'être* – and expansion itself was a cruel revealer of that loss.

This is the point at which theory stepped in to literary studies and the march of structuralism began in the 1950s, encouraged in America by the flight of scholars from Eastern Europe, and in Europe by the feeling that it was not only cities which needed rebuilding after the Blitz.

As academic life expanded, it acquired the panoply of any other growth area: resources, prestige, an internal self-validating structure of relationships, and an international dimension of the like hardly seen since the Middle Ages. This last feature has proved to be especially important in the production of a star-system which plays a major role in the theoretical heaven. Intellectual stars, sages and gurus have existed in Europe since Socrates twinkled at Alcibiades, of course, though never before in such confusing profusion and subject to such comprehensive media exposure. This is no bad thing. The star-system helps to stir the stagnating waters of the academic pool by encouraging an interest in new ideas through the disciples who gather round any new *maître à penser*. But there are dangers: it is easy to mistake the pool's ruffled surface for movement in the depths, and discipleship can turn into blind loyalty. Thinkers need critics, not fans; fashion's virtues include amusing gossip, not rational debate.

RLT has proved especially vulnerable to the dangers of the star-system because of its distinctive combination of obscure style and intoxicating utopian ideas. These ideas – the overthrow of bourgeois society, the absoluteness of the Text – are like hooks to catch unwary fish who suffocate in the unfamiliar atmosphere of radical discourse. The modern star-system demands drastic simplification: the identity of individuals with simple and distinctive concepts. That can be a virtue in politics: it is almost always a vice in academic affairs, disastrously so when combined with the sort of gratuitous subtlety which only strong minds can resist.

The problems are summed up in the career of Roland Barthes, king of media intellectuals. Barthes managed to go one beyond the star-system by turning theory into news. Having discovered that the only way to avoid following fashion is to make it, he sired and abandoned new 'sciences' of literature with all the gusto of a crazed cuckoo leaving others to pick up the pieces. He brought to theory a journalist's sense of publicity and a decorator's eye for effect. His strategy is to leave readers in breathless permanent pursuit, and academic interpreters stranded with one or another of his discarded doctrines like so many beached professorial whales. His work, his life and his reputation are High Comedy at its best, all written with the lightest of touches, an hilarious snook cocked at academic solemnity, a fine contribution to the gaiety of nations.

Barthes' texts add up to a thinly disguised autobiographical monologue – and how appropriate that the author of the Author's Death should be a narcissist whose only subject is himself! That is itself a perfect Barthesian paradox, an illustration of his own claim that literature is 'institutionalized subjectivity'. It is also a reminder that no coherent theory whatever can be extracted from his work. This is not in itself a criticism but it is a reproach to a writer who was always promising a comprehensive theory of criticism the day after tomorrow. The joke is on the people who believed him – the fish who swallowed this particular hook and laboured in vain to work out what it meant. And it points us once again in the direction of RLT's powerful mythological drive. That a comprehensive or totalizing literary theory is either possible or desirable in some remote future is perhaps the most potent – and the most unexamined – myth of all; and we must turn now to a consideration of how it could arise in the first place.

Historical Myths

As it happens, radical theorists themselves are keen to explain their position in historical terms, and they have devised two types of mythology to do so. The first is concerned with the distinctive evolution of literary studies over the last two or three centuries, the second with the longer perspective of Western cultural and political history.

Internal histories are founded for the most part on a myth of bringing order into chaos or its opposite: chaos revealed in the midst of apparent order. Structuralist and Marxist accounts take the first form, deconstructive and feminist explanations the second. According to the first myth, academic literary study (especially since the institutionalization of vernacular literature in the university a century ago) tells a story of growing awareness concerning its own rational underlying principles and their relationship to a wider intellectual context. What was originally a series of ramshackle buildings has now been given proper foundations according to a good groundplan.

The second myth explains that this is itself a myth: what literary studies presented to the world was an impressive facade which concealed an unlimitable sequence of rooms, now revealed to be such by the anti-scientific endeavours of feminist and deconstructive critics. No groundplan is possible, and any foundations must themselves be provided with foundations which must in turn etc. etc.

These two positions are well represented by two books published in the mid-1970s: Barthes' *The Pleasure of the Text* and Eagleton's *Criticism and Ideology*. Both are preoccupied with the critic's interpretative role, but whereas Barthes wants a kind of hermeneutic anarchy, determined by individual sensuous response to a general textuality, and both limited and facilitated by the ultimate impossibility of ever fixing meaning in its flight, Eagleton (then under the Althusserian influence) insists on a radical critical politics which installs the master-critic as guide. The contrast of hedonism versus discipline informs every aspect of the two texts from their messages to their textual character, the blissful belle-lettrism of Barthes in sharp contrast with Eagleton's stern jargon. One is reminded of the contrast between Wilde and Ruskin; and Barthes and Eagleton could well stand as the great aesthete and the great moralist of contemporary theory.

As this comparison suggests, the two approaches, so very different in outlook, can nevertheless be subsumed in the larger perspective of European cultural history. From this distance it is easy enough to see the striking similarities between Wilde and Ruskin, who share a common belief in the significance of art as a political and moral force.[2] The same is true of Barthes and Eagleton. And as with Wilde and Ruskin, their theoretical discourse often obscures or supersedes the art to which it is meant to draw attention, as though the critical homily had itself become the main object of our attention.

This is not new. What does mark Barthes – and more particularly Eagleton – out from their predecessors is their feeling, common in radical theory, that over the last half-century we really have reached a crucial turning point in human affairs, a stage which is historically unique, and within which literary theory is destined to play a vital role – more significant than the art it nominally points to. It represents, in a way difficult to formulate, a decisive increase or change in the quality of human consciousness, which is to be equated in the Hegelian-Marxist terminology of such matters, with a potential increase in human freedom and progress.

One characteristically ingenious combination of internal and external histories which dwells on this point is offered by Eagleton in a series of texts which, between them, construct a whole mythology of their own, most notably in *Literary Theory* and *The Function of Criticism*. Eagleton is a devotee of the *1066 and All That* school of Marxist critical history, all Good and Bad Things, and one's faith in his reliability as a guide is severely tested by his habit of taking large areas of critical consensus for granted. Nevertheless, this has the advantage of stimulus: Eagleton is a polemical writer and all the better for it. One senses that he doesn't take theory too seriously.

Inevitably enough, Eagleton links the emergence of literary criticism with the rise of the bourgeoisie, said to be in revolt against European absolutism at the end of the seventeenth century. In *The Function of Criticism*, capitalism's victory over feudalism (the political and economic consequence of the bourgeois revolt – but also, rather puzzlingly, its cause) is said to have brought to birth an intelligentsia which included both professional writers and gentleman amateurs, uniting them in the public sphere – a dubious concept Eagleton borrows from Habermas to suggest the free exchange of ideas founded not on authority but on the appeal to truth as reason, and famously embodied in Addison's metaphor of the Stock Exchange.

But bourgeois criticism, like all manifestations of capitalism, was characterized from the start by internal contradictions which gradually became more and more apparent over the next two centuries. At the heart of these contradictions was an illusory notion of universal reason – illusory because such a discourse is available only to those with the means to participate in it, and who therefore read back into it their own assumptions and predilections as universal traits, e.g., objectivity, rationality, individualism, personal freedom. The bourgeois critic is therefore the victim of his own ideology, just as the medieval theologian was – with the crucial difference that, whereas medieval theology corresponds to the hierarchical structure of feudalism, bourgeois criticism is self-contradictory, insofar as it postulates an illusory freedom which is just the opposite of the case. The public sphere, real enough to those who participate in it, is thus a fiction seen in the larger context of society as a whole.

This contradiction becomes painfully apparent when vernacular literature is institutionalized at university level, for only the attempt to construct a coherent intellectual programme in literary studies reveals it by revealing its own contradictions. Concentrating on England, Eagleton notes that whereas English achieved university recognition at the expense of the classical studies which formed the core of the liberal humanist education system – and with whose essentially amateur status the usurper identified; because it was a latecomer, having worked its way up through schools, training colleges and workers' colleges, it was also closely identified with the nascent radicalism (and vocational professionalism) of the underclass. Thus what Eagleton calls elsewhere The Rise of English neatly – and so conveniently – encapsulates the profounder class conflict surfacing at the end of the nineteenth century.

Once English (and presumably French, German, Italian? Eagleton doesn't say) was established after the First World War, this conflict emerged in a bitter rivalry between the traditionalist teachers who are said to have seen the subject as an inferior substitute for Greats, and the new *soi-disant* professionals who combined methodological austerity with the loftiest intellectual ambitions, out to create not merely a self-sufficient new discipline but *the* discipline – having imbibed enough Arnoldian liberalism to make them pine for Eng. Lit. as the core of a new university curriculum, apparently about to be dominated by natural science.

Eagleton has a good deal of fun at the expense of F. R. Lucas, Walter Raleigh, Q., and other worthies of the Oxbridge English schools, who are presented as literary winetasters and actual winebibbers bellowing patriotic slogans and ever ready to trample on women and the lower orders, but his real interest is in the St George who arrived to save the critical maiden by slaying these dragons, in the figure of F. R. Leavis.

This popular fairytale has been told too often to bear much repetition. Nevertheless I have had to sketch it here, if only because Leavis lurks in the background of all Anglo-Saxon radical theory and on him the whole of its mythical historiography reposes. For he is at once St George *and* the dragon: a slayer of the old orthodoxies, but himself the orthodoxy who must be slain again and again. In radical discourse he is the repressed who always returns, the contradiction which can be neither resolved nor rooted out – or so it seems. He is in Anglo-Saxon literary theory what Husserl is to continental radical philosophy: the phenomenologist whose Herculean attempt to found an entire discourse on subjective experience is the end of one epoch and the beginning of another. (Indeed, it is the comparison between Leavis and Husserl which allows Eagleton to slide silently from English to European criticism in *Literary Theory*.)

Eagleton's account of Leavis turns on his predecessor's paradoxical attempt to give literary studies educational and cultural hegemony by restricting their transmission to a narrow tradition taught by an elite corps of professional teachers and critics – the point at which Leavis most dramatically embodies Eagleton's thematic contradiction. By calling for a rigorous professionalism while remaining wedded to the amateur methodology of taste and intuition; by creating a critical aristocracy of the spirit in the name of saving the masses through high culture; by resisting theory while involuntarily exposing ever more clearly the mystified theoretical basis of his own work and the bourgeois tradition to which it belongs; by his insistence on the moral value of criticism at the expense of its political role; by his subscription to a naïve mimeticism; and by his confusion of personal taste and petit-bourgeois ideology with objective judgment and permanent human values – in all these ways Leavis exemplifies the contradictions of bourgeois society.

Once the cat was out of the bag, it was only a matter of time before it began to scratch holes in the critical edifice, unravelling neat notions of critical authority and the validity of a public sphere within which common values could be taken for granted. In this respect Leavis is both personally accountable but also symptomatic, for the logic (or non-logic) of his situation was just one form of a general stage in the development of Western capitalism, apparent in all areas of life in recurrent economic crises, spiritual malaise, collapse of moral authority, violent political upheavals and the sharp break in cultural traditions known as modernism. Thus the crisis in English was part of a worldwide crisis.

The story is familiar enough, but the appearance of theory gives a new twist to the dialectic. For once liberal humanism reaches a terminus in phenomenology, empirical criticism, social democracy, etc., the next stage is the intensive self-scrutiny which means revolution in politics and theory in criticism. Theory is thus a stage on the road to the new culture, as revolution is a stage on the road towards the new politics, and the advocates of permanent revolution are also inclined to support permanent theoretical revolution. Theory is part of a political process: at once the symbol of the liberal crisis and the means of overcoming it.

Eagleton's account of theory's appearance as a response to the internal contradictions of bourgeois criticism brings out well the three closely linked myths on which radical theory's self-history depends: the myths of crisis, culture and progress. Finding Marxist form in Eagleton, these are pervasive throughout radical theory because of its Hegelian foundations, and it is the Hegelian view of history, according to which a world-totality evolves in cycles, which is pervasive in theoretical writing.

There is no scope in this little book for close examination of what amounts to a whole mythology, but nor is there need for such comprehensiveness. Instead we can consider the whole boiling in one widely popular sub-myth which itself provides a major buttress for theory, i.e., the myth of modernism.

Modernism is generally supposed to mark a crucial turning point in the evolution of Western culture, a kind of collective nervous breakdown (a crisis, in fact) after which nothing was the same again. It is also often assumed that this cultural debacle corresponds to political, social and economic upheavals (the First World War, Russian Revolution etc.) in the same period. In short, modernism is a classic instance of all three myths: a moment which signifies progress from one cultural mode to another, while symbolizing a fundamental political realignment: the end of liberal democracy, bourgeois individualism and all the other fetishes of radical theory. It is therefore that theory's vital precursor, and there are good arguments for supposing that radical theory is little more than the working out of certain tendencies in modernist art.

Unfortunately, the empirical evidence (not that theory is much concerned with such things) is all against the view that modernism decisively changed Western culture. Take, for example, the question of realism, a bourgeois convention supposedly shown up as just that by modernist innovations in fiction. While experimental novels continue to be written (as they always were), they have not seen off the other kind. On the contrary, realism flourishes more vigorously than ever, having received a shot in the arm, not a death sentence, from the experiments of the early century which didn't kill realism, but merely encouraged us to widen our definition of it. The same might be said of liberal democratic institutions and the capitalist economy, which have undergone a remarkable revival in the last thirty years – to such an extent that Eastern Europe is currently moving away from all forms of collectivism, back to Western ideals of freedom, autonomy and subjectivity.

Ironically enough, this might be taken as confirmation of the very view I am challenging – namely that there is a close relationship between developments in all spheres of life and a total history within which they are inscribed, but it would be reckless to draw such a conclusion when, at the same time, the very intellectuals who advocate such a view are so vigorously resisting the changes in the Soviet system. On the contrary, what the evidence seems to point to is the difficulty of formulating a coherent historical explanation in Eagletonian terms of a progressive evolutionary pattern in cultural affairs. And indeed, it is worth remarking that Marx himself was sceptical of such enterprises, taking the view that art's relation to the economic base and the political superstructure is not a matter which will bear that much systematic investigation. Perhaps he was wiser than Hegel in this respect.

It is from within this triple mythology of culture, crisis and progress that an heroic view of the critic-as-theorist emerges, in succession to his nineteenth-century predecessor, the critic-as-moralist. But he emerges, by a delicious irony, to play exactly the same roles of guide, philosopher and sage, merely substituting politics for ethics. Who better to help us through the uncertainties of our time than the man trained to Read all the Signs of a Culture which now embraces everything from high art to low life? And who better to predict and explain each crisis in the historical cycle than the man learned in the intricacies of textuality – for who better than the professional exegete understands not only texts but the General Text of which they are the paradigm? Arm this man with the socialist objectives of liberty, equality and fraternity, and he becomes a member of the Management: those glorious creatures who will lead – or push – us into the future. This is a heady formula by means of which the critic can become at once more technically efficient and more socially useful: a highly desirable result in an age when literary criticism can appear increasingly trivial and undirected: and it is precisely the formula suggested by Barthes in the book from which I have taken the title of this chapter, *Mythologies*.

The academic popularity of that text owes a good deal to the great future it predicts for the critic – on condition that he renounces literary discourse in favour of ideological analysis and a semiological science of which such discourse would be a minor part. Barthes is frank about this, and about the role of cultural overlord he expects the critic to assume. This role may look to the sceptical reader like a recipe for Zhdanovism: under the influence of Nietzsche, Barthes came to much this conclusion himself, abandoning the pursuit of political correctness in favour of readerly bliss. Yet he never abandoned the project of a literary science, central to the structuralist enterprise. It is to a consideration of that project we now turn.

3

The Science of Literature

Newspaper readers of the older generation
will recall the sensational reports of his
arrest for *impersonating himself* . . .

'The science of literature (should it ever exist) . . .'[1] What is
structuralism and in what sense is it meant to be scientific?

These questions are not easy to answer and they are
complicated by a muddle about the difference between structuralism and semiology. Structuralism is an analytical method
based on the discovery of isomorphisms: structural similarities which recur from one text to another, underlying apparent differences. Instead of thematizing the features of a text
by discussing its content, the structuralist critic sets out to
compare configurations of features between texts. What
matters to him is not what this or that novel may be about,
but the conditions which make its meaning possible. Literature consists of the foregrounding or making explicit of such
conditions as structures, and it is the critic's business to locate
them. Aristotle's attempt to account for the effects of tragedy
in terms of a recurring pattern of elements is a fair example
of ur-structuralism.

But literary criticism is only one aspect of structuralism's
larger project, which is nothing less than the introduction of
order, method and sound epistemological foundations into
what are pre-emptively called the human sciences. It is a bid
to end what structuralists see as the dominance of subjectivity
in these human sciences in two forms: the ramshackle empiricism which supposedly reduces them to collections of
random observations which can hardly be dignified with the

name of 'science'; and the spectator theory of knowledge which is said to presuppose a naïve relationship between a body of objective facts and the individual consciousness of the observer who records them. Structuralists want to discredit both aspects of bourgeois criticism in all the relevant fields (literature, history, sociology etc.), replacing them with a universal and truly objective symbolic language – the language of structures. This project is as old as Aristotle, and enjoyed considerable popularity among eighteenth-century rationalists, but it has yet to amount to anything more than a few half-hearted attempts to make literary and historical studies more systematic.

There is, however, another way of looking at structuralism, not as a neutral cognitive science – a systematic way of explaining how we make sense of phenomena – but as a politicized ideological critique. It is in this sense that structuralism can be identified with the radical cause, and it comes about by focusing not on the methodology of the humanities but on their objective. Traditionally, this has been the study of cultural values (though not necessarily couched in this form): the explication and transmission of meanings and the significance attached to them. In this context the purpose of structural analysis has been seen as a continuation of idealist philosophy's project to reveal the difference between reality and appearance – more specifically, in this case, the difference between reality and bourgeois appearance. Structuralism thus regarded is a way of explaining how value-systems are constituted and – more significantly – how they can be dismantled.

The practical difference between the two approaches can be expressed in this way. A structuralist critic of the first sort writing about nineteenth-century fiction might be concerned with characteristic myths as recurrent structural motifs – the myth of the Fallen Woman, for example, which is invariably supported by a complex panoply of associations and plays an important role in the plots of many nineteenth-century novels.

The critic would show how this myth is articulated on different occasions, and what essential features there are in common between these occasions and the conventions to which they refer. His purpose would be to say something about the ways in which fiction, especially the three-volume novel, operates, and perhaps about the larger symbolic systems (thought of as mythologies) to which that fiction alludes.

The second sort of critic would treat the same material in very different fashion. His purpose would be to show how literary structures are used to support or undermine ideological prejudices. The myth of the Fallen Woman is important to him for what it tells us about the iniquities of sexual and class relations in bourgeois society – relations which prevail today to the extent that we either still naturalize the myth or regard it as a legitimate historical epoch. This critic would focus less on the relations between texts and more on the relations between literary structures and ideological realities.

Often enough, these approaches are run together. The essays in Barthes' *Image-Music-Text* are typical of the way in which structural analysis has been used as a basis for ideological critique. Unfortunately, while this project may be rhetorically effective it is logically incoherent. The two approaches are based on opposed principles, the first denying reference, the second affirming it. The first approach can properly be called structuralism because its purpose is not to assess the relationship between world and representation, context and text, or signifier and signified, but to identify and explain the recurrence of conventional features. Any correspondence between the structures thus described and the structure of any world they may or may not refer to is not only accidental but necessarily excluded from structural analysis which it would otherwise corrupt with empirical considerations.

The second approach, however, is not really structuralist at all, but a form of semiology – the science of signs whose whole purpose is the classification of representations. The second type of 'structuralism' thus involves us in a contradiction – or rather in a logical circle within which to identify a structure is already to interpret a sign, while to interpret a sign is already to limit a structure. Structuralism and semiology thus require one another as prior activities. We cannot analyse the structure until we have identified the sign which signifies it, and we cannot identify the sign until we have discovered the structure it represents. Or rather: we can only do so if we are ready to break into this circle on empirical grounds and admit that at some stage we just 'know from experience' what sign or structure we are looking for – an admission which makes nonsense of wilder claims to epistemological rigour.

It also causes serious methodological problems even in structuralist analyses without epistemological pretensions. In the work of Northrop Frye, for example, whose *The Anatomy of Criticism* predates most French literary structuralism by several years, it comprises an heroic attempt to define the laws of a literary system which would account for every historical and conceivable text. Frye's aim in critical theory corresponds to Lévi-Strauss's in anthropology: he wants to show that there is a hidden universal language into which all literature (or at least all Western literature) can ultimately be translated, and he does so by making of the critic a Shelleyan blend of scientist and poet. The scientist's task is to explain the rules according to which the literary system works, while the poet shows us how these rules embody our profoundest desires in what Frye calls myths of concern. Every text can thus be seen as a structure of conventions and as a value-system. Frye's problem is how to relate the two. It may well be the case, for example, that the four seasons correspond to certain human moods and certain literary modes. It may also be true that the binary oppositions in which Frye's scheme is grounded (spring/winter, comedy/tragedy etc.) are at the root of the ways in which we experience and represent the world; but it is a long step from possibilities to probabilities. Putting it crudely — how does Frye know that these structures correspond to those values, other than by virtue of the very literary experience his system is designed to explain? And is his system really the basis of a literary science? Or is it just another empirical shot at cataloguing literary texts? Frye refrains from lofty epistemological claims, but apparently thinks he has put literary studies on firm disciplinary foundations. Yet what are these foundations? What can one do with his literary system other than pigeonhole this or that text under the appropriate heading or argue about the arrangement of headings? In short, while Frye's *Anatomy* is an impressive achievement in itself, it does not seem to lead anywhere, trapped as it is within the circle of its own reasoning.

This dead end is recognized by Jonathan Culler in his classic study of the field, *Structuralist Poetics*. In the end, Culler believes, Frye's work amounts to little more than an elaborate rearrangement of literary classifications. He also recognizes its epistemological limitations which, though of no importance to criticism, are of vital significance for critical theory. For Culler believes that a true structuralist poetics must explain why and how literary texts affect us as they do, and it can only attempt this by shifting the emphasis from the cataloguing of texts to the cataloguing of readerly experience. This, in Culler's view, is where too many structuralist enterprises have gone wrong. In their legitimate flight from the horrors of bourgeois subjectivity, they have mistaken the structures of what is actually readerly experience for something 'in' the text. This is an easy mistake to make. As Genette, himself a distinguished structuralist critic, has remarked, in structural analysis it is often difficult to tell whether the structures described by the analyst were 'there' in the text waiting to be discovered, or whether he has invented them. Culler's approach will dispose of this problem. He proposes to attend not to texts but to interpretations. His aim is the codification of hermeneutic rules which will close the 'gap' in Frye's theory between literary conventions and value-systems by locating value in the ideological constitution of interpretation, thus uniting structuralism and semiology in a new literary science, which will also be a cognitive science.

Barthes has remarked that the basis of this new science will 'of course be linguistic. There is no reason not to try to apply such a method to works of literature.'[2] The tortuous syntax here may well make us uneasy. Does the breezy confidence of 'of course' really prevail over the double negative ('no reason not to . . .') to quell our doubts about the wisdom of founding new sciences in a field which is itself riven by complex arguments about its proper object of study? Perhaps this is not a problem for radical theorists, in whose book there is anyway only one important type of linguistics: the sort initiated by the Swiss scholar Saussure. Or rather – the sort which takes its cue from Saussure. For radical theorists are fond of citing this master's authority for their wilder claims without paying much attention to his own common-sense views. Thus Saussure's central hypotheses – that words signify concepts, not things, and that language is structured differentially (in terms of internal relationships) not referentially – are often taken to imply that language is the only reality, that it cannot refer to anything outside itself, or that we are trapped inside it. This view has acquired greater authority by linking Saussure with the Wittgensteinian notion that the limits of my language are the limits of my world.

But neither thinker denied the evident existence of an external world, nor the possibility of our knowledge of it, however oblique. Saussure was an old-fashioned realist who accepted language's referential function without question. Even if he hadn't, it is still not too difficult to work out that the autonomous functioning of a system (such as language) does not prevent that system from referring outside itself, as a simple experiment with numbers will show. One can also enquire why language should come into existence in the first place, if it is not to signify? Indeed, it can be said that signification is the defining characteristic of language. To be what it is a language – however simple or complex – must mean.

Part of the confusion here – and this is typical of the rows about linguistics referred to above – concerns the structuralist tendency to assume that language and code are the same thing, which they are not. A code is merely the vehicle of a language. Morse code, for example, is a simple binary system which says nothing in itself. And while it is the case that language is constituted from codes – conventional signifying systems – these codes do not exhaust it. On the contrary, English and French are capable of producing an infinite number of meaningful sentences from their limited codes. Culler is well aware of this point, and far too canny to tie his wagon to Saussure, though nodding respectfully in that master's direction. Instead he proposes to found his new science on Chomskyan linguistics, in particular the famous distinction between competence and performance.

Culler underlines the points of contact between Saussure and Chomsky. His main point – and the reason for his choice of linguistics as a basis for the new science – is that they both characterize language in terms of system and instance. In Saussure's case, this is a matter of contrasting *langue* (the linguistic system) with *parole* (any specific utterance drawn from that system). But, as Culler suggests, this model focuses our attention on the system. Chomsky's distinction between competence (a subject's mastery of the linguistic system) and performance (his ability to use it) emphasizes the role of the speaker – which, in Culler's terms, means the reader. Just as we talk of speakerly competence, so we can talk of readerly competence, i.e., the reader's mastery of the rules underlying any act of interpretation, which thus becomes analogous to a Chomskyan speech act. This approach has the added advantage of emphasizing our (usually) unconscious learning of rules, which are (at best) traditionally formulated as literary conventions. Thus a structuralist science of literature will not only be uncovering the rules which determine the meaning of texts: it will be contributing to a grand science of Man within which cognitive and psychic laws will also be fully explained.

Culler is cautious about such possibilities, in marked contrast to many of the theorists he writes about, and the contrast stirs a certain unease in this reader, immediately blurring the focus of the whole project. Culler's own aims are (comparatively) modest. He wants what his title proclaims: a structuralist poetics. But as we read on – and Culler ably demolishes the grander pretensions of his subjects – we cannot help wondering what will be left of the enterprise when he has finished, and what help it will give the critic above and beyond the inherited conventions and ad hoc systems to which every writer on literature has recourse. And by an ironic chance, the structure of Culler's own book reflects these doubts, when its last chapters take up the then (1974) emerging doctrines of deconstruction which were effectively to destroy the structuralist enterprise.

On the other hand, it is the grander pretensions of structuralism which have left their mark on radical theory, and Culler is perhaps more respectful than the structure of his own text, when it comes to dealing with them. Many of his subjects require more forceful demolition. Take, for example, Lévi-Strauss whose *Mythologiques* proved to be a seminal work in radical theory's own mythology. This text is founded on two highly dubious principles or assumptions: (1) that mankind is a psychic unity; and (2) that this unity is manifested in cultural phenomena. What these seem to mean taken together is that, in spite of practising widely different customs, human communities have the same individual and collective mental structures, and that these structures can be read off by the structural anthropologist who stands ready with his isomorphisms. But it is never clear whether Strauss is basing his analysis on his assumptions or deriving his assumptions from his analysis. An enormous amount of 'evidence' is accumulated, but its status remains uncertain and it rests on these dubious hypotheses, which call to mind Freud's rhetorical question to Einstein: 'Does not every science come in the end to a kind of mythology?'[3] Lévi-Strauss might put this the other way round: believing that we make unwarranted distinctions between Western civilization and so-called primitive cultures, he takes the view that tribal creation stories are no better and no worse than scientific cosmologies. They fulfil a cultural function. This suggests that Lévi-Strauss's own work belongs with his corpus of myths: it is itself a kind of mythology, its source a mystical view of universal humanity. From this point of view, structuralism itself appears not as a science but as a myth, and that is perhaps the best way to think of it.

Curiously, Lévi-Strauss himself does not take this line. Instead he follows the linguist Roman Jakobson, whose chance meeting with Lévi-Strauss in wartime South America was to have a powerful influence on the anthropologist in several respects. Especially important to him was Jakobson's faith in the possibility of 'an unbiased, attentive, exhaustive, total description of the selection, distribution and interrelation of diverse morphological classes and syntactic constructions'.[4] Substitute 'mythologies' for the last five words of this quotation and we have Lévi-Strauss's project in all its positivist glory. Jakobson believes that linguistic analysis can eventually reveal all the secrets of any literary text, however remote, and that these secrets will boil down to a limited number of grammatical and syntactic functions: the symmetries and contrasts which make the text what it is. Lévi-Strauss took Jakobson's phonemic and semantic analysis as a model for his discussion of myth, and shared his belief in the possibility of scientific completeness.

This belief is supported by two further points taken from Jakobson. First that the analyst should pay more attention to the form of an utterance than to its content. This is characteristic of structuralism. As Jakobson's colleague Mukarovsky put it, 'The function of poetic language consists in the maximum foregrounding of the utterance.'[5] Lévi-Strauss held that mythical language resembled poetic language, and that the form, style and structure of a myth counts for more than its manifest content. Secondly, he concluded that mythology, like language, has not only structure but grammar – that the grammar is, in a sense, the structure. This grammar is universal and unconsciously acquired: it is the communal inheritance which shapes our view of the world. To make it explicit is therefore to reveal the underlying psychic structures of mankind which it embodies. This – not the accumulation of empirical data – is the task of the anthropologist.

Lévi-Strauss's project is – to say the least – ambitious and it is characteristic of intellectual aspirations in the middle years of the century (in both the humanities and the sciences) to produce complete explanations of phenomena. The resulting surveys of myth are fascinating, but their theoretical coherence is, as we might expect, as dubious as comparable eighteenth-century projects for a Universal Science of Man. To some extent Lévi-Strauss is stymied by the very comprehensiveness of his project whose sheer tidiness renders it both suspect and arbitrary. There must also be doubts about the use of such a system. One commentator has remarked that in Lévi-Strauss's universe of myths, 'Everything is meaningful, nothing is meant',[6] but there is one exception to this rule: Lévi-Strauss's project itself, which reveals a drive to theoretical mastery at odds with the very material it presents. There is more than neutral cognitive science here. Though Lévi-Strauss is not a structuralist of the second type discussed at the beginning of this chapter, his work has the same didactic urge as its eighteenth-century models, the synoptic histories of Montesquieu and Voltaire. It may be that 'nothing is meant' in the myths Lévi-Strauss discusses, but his own myth – the myth of structural anthropology – is replete with purposeful meaning.

We can see the contrast at work very clearly in one brief

quotation. Drawing on Jakobson once more, Lévi-Strauss deploys the linguist's influential distinction between metaphor and metonymy in the following passage:

> If birds are metaphorical human beings and dogs metonymical human beings, the cattle may be thought of as metonymical inhuman beings and racehorses as metaphorical inhuman beings.[7]

Metonymy works by association, metaphor by substitution, so this passage seems to be saying that birds stand for human beings while dogs suggest them, and so on. However, the passage opens with a very characteristic 'If': Lévi-Strauss is offering a hypothesis, not an exhaustive Jakobsonian analysis. Certainly, everything here means something – but what is the significance of the meaning if 'nothing is meant'?

This question takes us to the crux of structural analysis, for of course everything *is* 'meant' – by the analyst himself. In this case, it is Lévi-Strauss who 'means' because it is he who finds (or rather, attributes) meaning in this complex scheme of binary oppositions. The universal language of myth he hopes to discover, can be discovered only in his own methods. Having already decided on the psychic unity of mankind, Lévi-Strauss looks for evidence to support his theory. Take, for example, his treatment of the Oedipus myth in different versions. Lévi-Strauss locates in these versions the same structure because he looks for comparable features – and he does this because he has already decided that comparable features are the important ones. This is a fundamental assumption of structuralism. But why should we share this assumption? Why should we not take the view that it is the differences between versions of the same story which constitute its real interest, as indicating the diversity of human psychic structures, which modify the same material even within a relatively small geographical and cultural compass? We can put this in another way by asking a question. If there really is a universal language of myth, who speaks it, other than Lévi-Strauss himself, and of what use is it except to bear out his own hypothesis?

Once again we encounter the paradox of structuralism, and in a peculiarly piquant form. For the very process of analysis raises questions about what structures are, where they are located, and what exactly we are analysing. Lévi-Strauss has set out to give an account of the universal psyche and ended by expressing only the structure of his own thought, recreating the world in his image.

The single most important contribution made by Lévi-Strauss and Jakobson to the development of structuralist critical theory is the notion that literature can be discussed as though it were a symbolic language with identifiable units of discourse and characteristic grammatical functions. Their successors were inclined to conclude from these discoveries that poetics can therefore be reduced to grammar, and that the critic's task is to analyse the basic units of literary discourse, just as the grammarian analyses the basic units of linguistic discourse. A number of critics followed this up in the 1950s and 1960s, among them Greimas, Todorov and Jakobson himself; and as we shall see in the following chapter, the project is still under way in deconstructive attempts to write a grammar of rhetoric, attempts which elaborate on Culler's demand for a poetics of reading.

This project was anticipated in the 1930s by scholars like the delightfully named Propp, who tried – in ways even Samuel Beckett couldn't parody – to catalogue the syntactical structures of Russian fairy stories in his *The Morphology of the Folk Tale*. Like many after him, Propp takes the sentence as the basic unit of sense, and he analyses narratives in terms of the functions within the sentence: subject (hero, heroine, villain etc.), predicate (their actions and what happens to them) and so on. This leaves him with thirty-one characteristic narrative units (which he calls 'functions'). Every tale contains some or all of these functions (slaying the monster, marrying the princess etc.) and always in the same order, and Propp suggests that they can be used to analyse any narrative.

One may well ask what the purpose of such analysis is from the literary critic's point of view? What, after all, is it telling us about? These questions become even more pressing when we discover that Propp's successors have 'improved' on his theory by reducing the number of functions. A. J. Greimas, hoping to arrive at a universal grammar of narrative via a semantic analysis of sentence structure, turns the seven 'spheres of action' in which Propp placed his thirty-one functions to three pairs of binary oppositions, pairing off six 'actants' who generate all stories:

> Subject/Object
> Sender/Receiver
> Helper/Opponent[8]

As Raman Selden has pointed out,[9] this is more authentically structuralist than Proppism is, by virtue of the fact that it incites the critic to compare relations, not entities, but it is still not good enough for Todorov[10] who hopes to systematize the whole business even further. Perhaps in time we will reach the logical terminus of this tendency: the analysis of all narratives in terms of one binary opposition. Gerard Genette's essay on the 'Frontiers of Narrative'[11] has already got it down to three: narrative and representation, narration and description, narrative and discourse. These distinctions can, in fact, be illuminating, but it is difficult to see anything especially structuralist about them – or anything very new. The first refers to the difference between authorial narration and imitation of a character, and can be found in Aristotle. The second distinguishes between story-telling and description and can be found in Fielding and elsewhere; and the third distinguishes between anonymous narrative and dramatic monologue, and can be found theorized in the prefaces of Henry James (as, indeed, can all the others). But at least

Genette's categories are heuristically useful for the critic. The same cannot be said of Propp, Greimas and Todorov, who all appear to be contributing to a Lévi-Straussian ideal of universal grammar. Their work therefore belongs more to linguistic theory than to literary theory. More to the point, it is of little help in the attempt to construct a structuralist poetics as a theory of reading, because what Propp, Greimas and Todorov give us are not rules but conventions. It is not a rule that all stories contain elements from a given list, merely an empirical observation of conventional practice. And even if Greimas is right about the basic patterns which recur in all narrative, this too cannot be regarded as a rule. In other words, this kind of structuralism may be helpful in providing us with an exhaustive catalogue of narrative conventions used in the past, but it cannot predict either how they will occur in the future or how we will read them. The universal grammar of literature, like the universal language of myth, is no more than a personal tidying-up job on existing texts, which may be more or less useful according to taste.

For what structuralist critics are inclined to forget is that literature – and language, for that matter – are not simply symbolic codes in the sense that, say, morse code is. For one thing, they evolve historically and a good deal of our understanding of both depends on context. And not only are language and code very different things. A language cannot be reduced to a code, any more than it can be reduced to a grammar. The same is true of literature: grammar is one way of talking about language, and it seems reasonable to suggest that it might also be one way of talking about literature. But that is all it is: one way, not an ultimate explanation or a body of legislative rules. The mistake structuralist critics make is not in attempting to grammatize literature but in hoping that the results of their efforts will somehow take priority over other ways of talking about it. There is all the difference in the world between expanding the vocabulary of criticism and deciding to replace it unilaterally.

This point was well understood by the dominant figure in structuralist criticism, Roland Barthes, even though he took a mischievous rhetorical pleasure in occasionally pretending to be a stern revolutionary intent on sweeping away all the horror of bourgeois criticism in favour of the new structuralist regime. But perhaps Barthes knew himself well enough to know that he wasn't really a structuralist at all, except when it suited the occasion. His real dedication was to a dandified variety of critical pluralism in which all flowers were encouraged to bloom so long as they were bright enough.

That, at least, is how it often appears. But as we shall see, Barthes was a complex figure for whom being consistent, high on the list of academic virtues, was a matter of no importance; and it is equally reasonable to see his attitude to criticism not as generously pluralist but as disturbingly narrow. In *Criticism and Truth*, for example, he distinguishes between reading, science and criticism. Reading is the projection and fulfilment of individual desire in the interpretation of the text. Science is the attempt to explain the nature and function of literature and to provide rules for interpretation (what Culler means by structuralist poetics). This leaves criticism with one role only: the attribution of determinate meanings to the text. The critic, in other words, is simply there to explain what happens if we apply Marxist or Freudian or phenomenological or any other rules to this or that text, and critics can be arranged in schools accordingly. Now while there is some truth in this as a description of what many academic critics actually do — applying this or that idea to texts much as a chemist might apply a substance to a compound — it ignores almost all the interesting and important aspects of critical activity in favour of a simple mechanical operation. It also assumes that this operation *is* simple: that there is no more to it than putting paradigms to texts and waiting to see what comes of it. This has the effect of subordinating criticism to science, i.e., theory, by making the critic a technician who experiments in the literary lab. with the discoveries of better men.

One consequence of such subordination is the abolition of the critic's traditional roles within the academy as a transmitter of cultural values, and outside it as an arbiter of taste. At the same time, the scientist/theorist is appointed to fill these roles and more, by virtue of his status as a master semiologist: an interpreter of cultural signs, as described in the concluding essay of *Mythologies*. Not that such theorists will simply take over the educational and aesthetic functions of criticism, of course: their task is to demonstrate the arbitrariness of all values and all tastes, not to confirm one or another. That will be left to readerly desire, which always turns out to be Barthes' ultimate transcendental value.

The paradox of such a position is that Barthes himself was neither a theorist nor (merely) a reader, but a critic in the full-blown old-fashioned sense: an arbiter of taste, a transmitter of values, part pedagogue, part scholar, part entertainer, part mountebank – above all an amateur. And for all his disquisitions about theory, his work – even in the dottier reaches of *S/Z* – remains firmly in the tradition of critic as mediator: one who stands between public and writer on behalf of both. How does it come about that Barthes is the embodiment of everything he rejects?

No doubt the reason is partly the need to react against the very influences which formed him, to assert independence, to strike attitudes, to pretend to a radicalism weaker than it seems – and these motives must always be taken into account in any discussion of RLT. They are not illegitimate, but we need to be inoculated against them. But there are particular circumstances in French academic and intellectual life which engender the paradox of the institutionalized rebel. These circumstances are evident in exactly the essays which pose as a demolition of the intellectual traditions to which Barthes himself belongs, in particular *Criticism and Truth* and 'The

Two Criticisms' and 'What Is Criticism?' collected in *Critical Essays*.

The demolition is apparently achieved in the name of structuralism in particular, and a more scientific approach to literary studies in general. In practice it amounts to little more than cocking a brilliant snook at the academic establishment – a laudable activity but hardly the basis of a new science. In all three texts Barthes deploys his favourite rhetorical opposition (this is half the battle) between what he variously calls traditional, academic, positivist or bourgeois criticism, and the new theoretical science – or, as it turns out, sciences. For the reader is immediately struck by the fact that Barthes opposes traditional etc. criticism not only to structuralism but to a whole range of new 'sciences' including Marxism, psychoanalysis and existentialism. The argument here is not simply against the old methods – which are even allowed to have acceptable features – but against their claim to what a later Barthes would have called cultural hegemony. His objection to established critics is their appropriation of cultural authority, identified with the political authority of the state and enforced through schools, universities, text-books, an approved syllabus, professional journals, conventional scholarly practices, and above all the grand academies and institutes appointed to guard the purity of French national culture. In the guise of objectivity, lucidity and clarity proclaimed as the supreme literary and intellectual virtues, all these institutions continue the repressive regime of bourgeois society which defines what objectivity, lucidity and clarity are, using them as yet another means to exclude the proletariat from participation in that cultural and political power to which knowledge (also defined by the bourgeoisie) is the key.

This is a form of the ideological critique outlined at the beginning of the chapter, and Barthes supports it with attacks on the farce of French professional life. The elements of the comedy are familiar from Aristophanes onwards: stuffy dons patronizing the scholarship of others while allowing themselves outrageous intellectual licence and promoting their personal views under the banner of objectivity, when these views amount to no more than a repetition of bourgeois delusions. Having latched on to this stereotype, Barthes was naturally delighted when it materialized in the form of Professor Raymond Picard's attack on him as a fraud in a famous essay, *Nouvelle critique ou nouvelle imposture?*

Picardian critical theory, according to Barthes, believes in the possibility of correct readings of texts by means of scrupulous reference to the words on the page, the biographical and historical context in which they were produced, and common-sense criteria of verisimilitude and human nature. The scholar's job is to establish a good text, the critic's to explain it. There is little room for theory. Language, history, intention and interpretation are problematical only insofar as there may be a shortage of appropriate factual information to sustain them: these are matters of scholarship. Any other approach to criticism is subjective (bad) or ideological (very bad).

Barthes has little difficulty in disposing of the Picardian 'theory' of criticism, though the reader may notice that it is surprisingly close to his own. Both writers assume that the critic's job is simply to interpret the text: they differ only about the status of the theoretical model or models to be used. Nor does Barthes reject the claims of historical scholarship which are unacceptable to what Umberto Eco has called the ontological structuralist, that is the structuralist for whom the genesis of texts is an irrelevance. Instead, he tries to show that Picardian criticism's claims to objectivity involve it in contradictions, because the criteria according to which this objectivity is to be judged are – like the concept itself – historically and ideologically conditioned. Historical criticism is itself an historically grounded phenomenon – not, as Picard assumes, a universally valid practice. In the same way, Picard's simple theory of representationalism (the text reflects the world) betrays a failure to understand that the concept of mimesis has itself evolved historically, while his reliance on so-called external objective evidence (whether historical or biographical) neglects to enquire into the status of that evidence, which is, like the work itself, textually transmitted and therefore subject to the same vagaries of interpretation. In other words, we need to interpret the evidence by which we reconstruct the text as much as the text itself. These are all valid criticisms of Picard and the school of criticism he represents, though their theoretical validity is not necessarily matched in practice: whatever the weaknesses of his critical theory (or lack of it), it may turn out that Picard has interesting, important and valid things to say about Racine (the occasion of his quarrel with Barthes) just as Barthes may, either because of his theory or in spite of it.

It is not, however, Picard's theory or non-theory which is really at stake here. What Barthes wants to take issue with is Picard's insistence on the possibility of what his attacker calls univocal interpretation, i.e., the belief that there is one correct reading of every text, and that all readings approximate to it. This delusion produces what Barthes calls a-symbolia: a blindness to the plurality of the text, its manifold, even infinite possible meanings. Univocal interpretation in criticism is one aspect of the bourgeois state's claim to embody absolute standards of reason and justice, and Barthes' plea for hermeneutic freedom is therefore also a plea for political liberation.

It is at this point that serious doubts begin to creep in. It may be true that in France there is a close link between political and cultural institutions: that the state effectively sanctions what can be read and how it is to be understood. Certainly, the strong centralizing tendencies of French society are an historical fact, and this has no doubt played a part in shaping French literature and criticism from the late seventeenth century onwards. But it is this very circumstance which has permitted and even encouraged the emergence of rebels within the system as an integral part of it, from Voltaire to Derrida; and which has given these rebels a degree of cultural authority and public regard unimaginable in Anglo-Saxon countries, where intellectuals, rebellious or otherwise, remain either suspect or ignored. Rebellion is a naturalized activity in French society: it is part of the institution.

For this reason, rebels are perhaps inclined to overrate both the absolute ideological power of the state and their own significance in opposing it. They behave as though they were in Stalinist Russia – or at least in the France of Louis XIV. The conflict between official institutions (from governments to the literary syllabus taught in schools) and those who challenge them is dramatized, and the drama is supported by the mythology of a revolution inaugurated by enlightened intellectuals. 1789 is rerun over and over again. By the same token, those in authority are inclined to take their office too seriously. And so we get a Barthes and a Picard. The two are symmetrical, they are playing the same game. For Barthes' attempt to replace 'human nature' and verisimilitude as critical criteria with their opposites is just as dogmatic as Picard's insistence on univocal readings and scholarly correctness.

Nor is Barthes' critical pluralism the libertarian creed it seems. Like Picard, he wants to enforce an ideological view of criticism by excluding certain possibilities – namely, all the approaches valued by Picard and those like him. We should not allow Barthes' justified comedy at Picard's expense to obscure this point. Dogmatic libertarianism – the insistence that we shall all be free to do as we like (with certain exceptions) – is no better than dogmatic authoritarianism. And indeed it can be worse when, as in this case, it blithely ignores the fact that the plural critical viewpoints Barthes is so keen on come from somewhere and are going somewhere. They have origins in beliefs and they have consequences. Otherwise they are merely trivial. There is no interest whatever in a Marxist, existentialist, structuralist etc. interpretation of a text as such. It was one of structuralism's major weaknesses to assume that interpretations could somehow float free, forgetting that they only make sense in context. Thus Picard's approach – whatever one thinks of it – is logical on the assumption that most people share common-sense views about human nature, mimesis and reference, though he pushes critical authority too far. But the proper alternative is not a Barthesian free-for-all in which everyone cultivates their own hermeneutic paradigm, for the simple reason that there can only be meaningful paradigms when there is a degree of interpretive consensus available. The alternative is to move the critical emphasis away from interpretation, to relegate the hermeneutic activity to a more modest role within criticism generally. This is precisely what structuralism appeared to be doing, until it became clear that the provision of general invariant abstract rules for the reading of literary texts is quite simply an impossibility.

Had Barthes been less exclusively concerned with the literary and political situation in France – a common failing among French intellectuals – he might have noticed sooner that interpretation is not the solution to the problems of contemporary criticism. His attack on Picardian univocalism may have shivered timbers in Paris in the 1950s and 1960s, but it would hardly have raised an eyebrow in Cambridge or Yale, where the problem was not hermeneutic exclusiveness but hermeneutic authority. What troubled Anglo-Saxon critics in the mid-century was the sheer proliferation of conflicting interpretations of every conceivable text. The critical pluralism Barthes pleaded for already existed – and how. For despite the efforts of Leavis and his like to establish criticism as a serious discipline, and despite the enormous numbers of undergraduates studying it, 'English' was in the doldrums, demoralized on the one hand by the postwar standing of the natural sciences, and on the other by the increasing repute of the human sciences. As an academic discipline it had long threatened to disintegrate into two unjoinable halves: scholarship and interpretation; and ambitious academics were reduced to a choice between editing texts and producing yet another reading of Langland.

That, at least, is how structuralists presented the situation when they offered to remedy it at a stroke by introducing method into literary studies, thus raising them to the dignity of a science by uniting the scholarly and interpretive functions in the notion that the literary structure is a proper object of attention for both. Even better, structuralist claims that we understand and even constitute reality through our representations of it, suggested that literature, as our culture's major form of self-representation, might aspire to the central cultural role dreamed of for it by Arnold and Leavis. Structuralism thus promised to combine the glamour of science in an age of technological optimism, with the hope of the humanities in an age of political pessimism. It would reform society in ways humanist scholars could only dream of. No wonder its appeal was so potent, if so brief.

For hungry postgraduates in expanding universities, this noble aim had all sorts of useful by-products: restoring their prestige, stimulating jaded palates, providing new areas of study, and arming them with weapons against the old fogies who stood in the way of promotion – which was, after all, tantamount to standing in the way of human progress. For weren't these professorial fathers and grandfathers – the Leavises and Arnolds of their time – hopelessly compromised by that effete liberalism (occasionally masquerading as socialism) which had failed to stand up to the dictators and allowed two bestial wars which made a farce of their lofty humanist principles? And weren't they pathetically amateurish into the bargain – would-be gentlemen who wished they were in Oxbridge tasting literature and wine in equal quantities and with equal interest? It was time to sweep away both their politics and their criticism, and to replace them with a discipline which was scientific, radical and, above all, professional.

Soon a swelling band of postgraduates was at work,

discovering structures in everything from Kafka to cake-decorating – but what was the result? Not, alas, a new order, a mathematically beautiful critical model which explained everything, but more and yet more interpretations. The solution had turned into the problem. It seemed that structuralism was not an analytic key but a machine for producing more texts, and it wasn't long before its grand scientific pretensions had dwindled into either banal pseudo-sociological reflections on how advertisements and television programmes work, or polite chapters in surveys of literary theory.

But by that time – the early 1970s – Barthes had moved on. He no longer needed structuralism, and perhaps he never had. It was just another briefly useful mirror in his long engagement with himself. In retrospect it is clear that, beneath all the chopping and changing, he remained what early influences had made him. Under the guidance of Sartre and Merleau-Ponty, existential phenomenology dominated the French avant garde in the postwar period. Existentialism appealed to the romantic, rebellious, solitary side of Barthes: it allowed him to adopt a stance of permanent opposition. Phenomenology, the philosophy of consciousness according to which each subject builds up his picture of reality in creative acts of cognition, also has an heroic ring to it. Significantly, both philosophies can be seen as ultimate destinations – or dead ends – of the tradition which begins with Descartes' postulation of individual self-consciousness as the starting-point of knowledge. In other words, existential phenomenology is the most refined form of that bourgeois individualism to which Barthes and his colleagues claim to be opposed. It focuses everything on the individual, epistemologically, ethically and politically; and its literary derivatives are concerned with the individual's role in reconstituting the meaning of the text as an act of creative cognition, which is precisely Barthes' preoccupation in his later work. So the irony is that he ended up by espousing what he began by rejecting. Structuralism, Marxism and the rest are abandoned in a nakedly individualist hedonism – the subject pleasure of the text.

This evolution makes sense if we remember that the dominant motif of Barthes' career is himself. His best book – the brilliant *Roland Barthes by Roland Barthes* – is a complex series of reflections in which he constantly tries to catch himself unawares, as it were: to look at himself as though he were someone else, while remaining conscious of the impossibility of such a task. This is phenomenology at its most exquisitely refined. The same is true of his critical career, whose proper theme is not literature but Barthes. And like Narcissus, Barthes' fascination with himself is complemented by a powerful drive to escape being trapped at all costs – even by himself. As he pointed out, his work is dominated by the urge to formulate dogmas (he calls them *doxas*) which are then immediately abandoned. This has the advantage of allowing him to evade the consequences of any critical doctrine. By another irony, the man who dismissed taste as a bourgeois mystification is thus the ultimate aesthete, but the object of his aestheticism is neither texts nor (as one critic has suggested) theories of literature, but himself posing as a theorist. For Barthes can never quite believe in any of the doctrines he espouses, even while he expounds them. There is always this other consciousness in him which knows that the Barthes who is at present discoursing on, for example, structuralism, is a Barthes who has forgotten the ultimate truth: that all knowledge, like self-knowledge, is ultimately in flight – that we can never finally know anything, except the fact that we don't know it. This is the one unvarying *doxa* which informs all Barthes' work and it is the theme of his own critical dogmatism.

To make the paradoxical process of knowing that we don't know work, there have to be two minds in every critic: the one that doesn't know and the one that knows the other doesn't know. The first is an unsophisticated chap who believes in this or that and conscientiously tries to do his critical duty. The second is a brilliant cynic who knows that his twin is on a hiding to nothing, that life is short and chaotic, and that one had better take the pleasures which present themselves. The first believes in reason, the second in desire. The first critic, in short, is a Jekyll, the second a Hyde. Barthes' Jekyll is a serious fellow: sensitive, scholarly, politically committed. He writes at first – see *Writing Degree Zero* (1953) – under the influence of Marxism and existentialism. This text proposes to explain the structure and history of literature in rational terms. But then Hyde begins to show his head – and Hyde is out for satisfaction. At first Jekyll puts up a fight. In *Mythologies* (1957) the two struggle for mastery. Hyde has the best of it in the first part of the book, a series of jazzy essays on aspects of French life; but Jekyll reasserts himself in the long, final chapter, which attempts to put the essays in a theoretical context, asking us to believe that they are serious forays into semiological analysis. Even so, we can hear Hyde's laughter rippling through the gaps in the argument. The two continue to fight it out in *Criticism and Truth* (1966) and *Critical Essays* (1964), but gradually Hyde gets the upper hand, and by the time of *S/Z* (1970) he has won the battle so convincingly that he can persuade Jekyll that they are really in complete agreement. Together they produce in *S/Z* their ultimate paradox: a lengthy, enormously detailed pseudo-scholarly demonstration that all our knowledge of the text (in this case a short story by Balzac) only confirms that we have no knowledge of it. Thus are the critic's two personalities – the one that doesn't know and the one that knows the other doesn't know – united. After this, Hyde has it all his own way. Having established himself under the mask of Jekyll's attempts to construct a scientific theory of criticism, he is now free to blow his cover and to dispose of Jekyll altogether. *The Pleasure of the Text* (1973) is entirely Hyde's own work, but he cannot resist a final contemptuous fling at

Jekyll. This book, which celebrates the absolute power of readerly desire in interpretation, is still couched as a theory, but true to Hyde's principles it is an anti-theoretical, anti-foundationalist theory based on the notion that readerly desire exceeds all hermeneutic laws. Jekyll – who did not know that he did not know – has been vanquished by Hyde.

But this narrative is not only the story of Barthes' career and the careers of his professorial imitators who pose as Hydes but are really Jekylls at heart. It is also a parable of one major recent development in theory, away from the scientific, foundationalist pretensions of structuralism, towards the anti-scientific, anti-foundationalist principles of deconstruction, which is based on Hyde's discovery that there is no escape from interpretation. For even when Jekyll the structuralist has analysed a text, it turns out that whatever structures he discovers are also signs. Jekyll, it seems, must always turn into Hyde whatever he does. But what happened to Hyde's triumph we shall discover in the next chapter.

4

The Bliss of Ignorance

Like most of de Selby's theories, the ultimate
outcome is inconclusive.

The foundational pretensions of structuralism broke on the
rock of interpretation. It transpired that poetics and grammar
can themselves be seen not only as interpretive models but
also as rhetorical forms, and as such, susceptible of further
interpretation ad infinitum, by the simple means of changing
their context. At best, a literary grammar can provide only
conventional codes, not rules. As we shall see, this has not
prevented critics such as Paul de Man from attempting to
turn criticism into a grammar of rhetoric, but it has forced
them to retreat to pragmatic grounds. They now call their
activities strategic, not scientific. The dominant strategy of
the last two decades has been deconstruction. It comes in
many forms, but its elements are a vital part of the RLT
formula.

Like structuralism, deconstruction has methodological and
ideological aspects, and the relationship between them is
similarly vexed. Derrida, for example, alternates between
suggesting that his writing 'leaves everything as it is' because
no theoretical discourse, however comprehensive, is ever
more than a contextually determined instance; implying that
his ultimate goal is nothing less than the transformation of
society through ideological and educational critiques; and
hopping between the two. Thus deconstruction is sometimes
seen as an internal strategy, a method of criticizing literary
(and other) texts in terms of the technical and conceptual
traditions to which they belong. At other times, it appears

that these traditions extend to cultural and political areas (summed up as 'ideology') and that the internal strategy is a way of revising all our most fundamental value-terms along Nietzschean lines of a revaluation of all values. Thus, in a way, deconstruction has foundational aspirations comparable to structuralism's, except that its purpose is not to locate the foundations of knowledge but to show that there aren't any.

The example of Nietzsche's combative but ironic approach, and his insistence that we relativize our notions of truth, are crucial to deconstruction, as both Derrida and de Man testify. Nietzsche is also one model for Derrida's tactical refusal to be pinned down. It is not easy, in either case, to know how to respond to this sort of teasing, or what to make of it; and the consequence is that deconstructors tend to make anything they like of it, from a pure textual aestheticism – a kind of hedonistic pleasure in the free play of endless verbal associations – to a programme for full-blown revolution. Often enough – as in certain varieties of feminism – the first is offered as a means to (and the end point of) the second. The problem with deconstruction is exactly the problem for bourgeois criticism: it deteriorates with the greatest ease either into unbridled subjectivity or into the mere repetition of certain formulas derived largely from Derrida himself.

Derrida's view of the relationship between methodology and ideological critique is determined by his belief that there is no objective standpoint from which value-systems can be impartially reviewed. This has become a commonplace in our own time, and deconstruction can legitimately be regarded as a form of dogmatic scepticism. In such a context the critic's task is not the pursuit of truth but the always relativized evaluation of all discourses including – and primarily – his own. This does not mean that no discourses are better than others, only that better and worse are themselves values determined in context, not in relation to an absolute external standard. Derrida anticipates the simple objection to his claims – that he must himself have some starting-point for his argument, some grounds to which he can appeal – by suggesting that the appeal for epistemological grounds only requires a further appeal: we need grounds for our grounds, and so on. He claims (rather dubiously) to have no particular authority, but merely to be engaging in the endless dialogues which are philosophy and literary criticism – dialogues which move not forward, but in circles bounded by our limited range of terms and concepts. The attempt to escape 'metaphysics', i.e., foundational terms, is futile: all we can do is scrutinize our discourses with maximum vigilance (a favourite word).

Within such a sceptical scheme the main link between critical methodology and ideological critique is the idea of the institution. This is one way out of the collapse into subjectivity. Interpretations are potentially limitless because their contexts are limitless, but in practice this is not the case, because the languages which make interpretation possible (the language of New Criticism, for example, or the language of deconstruction itself) are determined by complex institutional structures which provide a limited number of contexts. These include everything from the psycholinguistic structure of the mind to the material conditions of higher education, but they are dominated by the rhetorical patterns of language itself, for it is in language that the two sides of the deconstructive project (critical methodology and ideological critique) meet. Language is both the means through which that project is made possible and the discourse in which cultural and political values are most profoundly – and therefore most elusively – embodied. Among linguistic forms, literature is the most complex and the most accessible. And it is not only in literature that we find our most sophisticated self-representations: those representations provide a pattern for what we do elsewhere – in other intellectual domains (philosophy, history etc.) and in our daily lives. Language and literature are therefore deconstruction's institutional paradigms and its means of saving itself from the collapse into subjectivity and scepticism.

These paradigms derive from axioms – and although deconstructors claim to be wary of doctrine, they generate their own dogma, in line with Derrida's assertion that there is no escape from metaphysics. Their tortuous syntax often obscures both this point and their unsurprising tendency to deploy these axioms as though they were immune to their own sceptical origins, but there is no reason to suppose that deconstruction is doing anything radically new. It is interesting as an attempt to reformulate scepticism in more detailed forms than has hitherto been the case – an attempt logically doomed to self-contradiction. Derrida's strategy – and the strategy of deconstruction in general – is to propose the incorporation of such contradiction into the scheme by accepting that all discourses, including his own, are paradoxical. The chief effect of this in literary terms is to destroy the idea (held by both New Critics and structuralists) that the literary text is a unity with a coherent form, while holding to the (New Critical/structuralist) view that the text's relationship to the world it apparently represents is problematic. These moves in turn render the traditional vocabularies of criticism (be they Aristotelian modes of character, plot and theme, or New Critical modes of irony, ambiguity and tension) redundant, because their vocabularies all depend either on presumptions of mimetic authenticity (Aristotle) or autotelic coherence (New Criticism). Given the fact that most critical vocabularies come somewhere between the two, combining formal and mimetic commentary, deconstruction hopes to undermine both approaches with one blow.

This blow is struck in the name of interpretation, on the grounds that critical vocabularies which think they are accurately describing literary texts are in practice interpreting them, and it is legitimated by reference to deconstruction's basic axioms: (1) that meaning is both unstable and contextual, and (2) that literary texts are part of a huge network of inter-referential discourses. There is, as Derrida puts it, nothing outside the text. Except to the dottier practitioners of the cult, this does *not* mean that there is no external world, only that our knowledge and experience of that world (if we can be held to have any) are constituted in the textuality of discourses, i.e., that in order to know or perceive anything, there has to be a medium within which to know or perceive it. This is the Kantian doctrine, that there is no unmediated knowledge, expressed in terms of a deconstructive theory of reading. Interpretation is potentially limited not only because each interpretation of a text is a new version of a text, but is itself a new text, ready to be interpreted.

This has serious implications for the critical models discussed in Chapter 1. If every reading of a text is already an interpretation, how can there ever be identity of meaning in the communication between writer and reader? And how can the writer know his own text, except by reading, i.e., interpreting it? As de Man puts it, interpretation involves 'being as rigorous a reader as the author had to be in order to write . . . in the first place'.[1] It seems that readers and writers alike are involved in a seamless web of textuality. Everywhere they look there is more text to be interpreted, and more interpretations generate – more text.

There is no way out of this web, but the hopelessness of the critic's predicament tangled up in it is not quite what it seems. True, critics are merely readers, like other men, and as de Man again puts it, the equivalence between critic and reader has become 'a commonplace of contemporary literary study'.[2] It might seem that the professional authority conferred on them by mastery of their specialized vocabularies has vanished. But this is not the case. For one thing, as we have noted, deconstruction has its own specialized vocabulary to take the place of the old ones – a vocabulary which is far more arcane than anything previously imagined; while for another, literature retains, even enhances, the privileged cultural position it had under the old liberal humanist regime by virtue of designation by deconstruction as not just one signifying practice among many, but as *the* practice: the major means by which Western societies have traditionally represented reality to themselves. Once representation is thought of as constitutive, not imitative, rhetorical analysis becomes an even more important skill than it was before. The critical function which compared texts with the world vanishes, taking with it the view that criticism is no more than rationalized common sense. The critic becomes a specialist – what one commentator has called a textuary,[3] an expert in the decoding of textual paradoxes. Thus the Barthesian master-semiologist is resurrected in a new form. His task is not now to reveal the truth behind ideological appearances but to show that there are *only* appearances. When the hero of Stoppard's *Travesties* removes his dressing-gown to reveal another dressing-gown, he shows himself a true decon-structor.

Some of the problems with the deconstructive scheme were hinted at in the previous chapter. The idea that language is a complete, self-referential system does not entail the view that it cannot refer outside itself, and the historical evolution of language points to the contrary view: that words do adapt themselves, if not to things then to concepts. Nor, even if we accept it, does the deconstructive doctrine of the sign – that the interpretation of one always leads to another ad infinitum – necessarily affect our interpretive practice: in reality – even in academic reality – interpretations are limited at any one time to a few alternatives. We may agree in principle that a text can mean an infinite number of things: its actual meanings are limited, though not prescribed in detail, by the context. Indeed, this is a point Derrida himself makes when he announces that for all practical purposes we will go on treating the world in the common-sense, realistic way we always have. There is no reason in his scheme of things why this mode of behaviour should not cohabit easily with the idealist doctrines of deconstruction – or so he would seem to imply. It is merely a misguided desire for consistency which makes us want to establish – say – philosophical reasoning and gardening on identical epistemological principles. But such ingenuousness, though it may help Derrida when argued into a corner, is no comfort to those who think that literature (and philosophy and history) are representations of reality, and that some texts are absolutely better than others. This is not a solution to the problem, only an accommodation. Nor does it get round the difficulty of reference, which is simply put on one side in favour of difference. The critic is meant to exclude all discussion of literature's relationship to the world, concentrating instead on its textual and intertextual status. In consequence, the critic's technical authority is expanded, and his cultural dominance enhanced, while his scope is reduced. The price literature pays for its exaltation in some forms of deconstruction is thus a complete loss of relevance in the form of the traditional reasons for that relevance, i.e., its power to confront us with convincing pictures of reality. The critic pays his share of that price and the results are familiar: an increase in the intensity and complexity of critical texts, and a decrease in their breadth and accessibility.

The problems involved in these changes are apparent in the work of Paul de Man. De Man is no radical. On the contrary, though exercised by the ethical issues at stake in the texts he discusses, he never fails to pay homage to his formalist origins. The theme of his most interesting book, *Allegories of Reading*, is precisely the relationship between formalist and ideological criticism discussed in terms of reference and difference. But his freedom from the dottier excesses of deconstruction committed by some of his colleagues – Geoffrey Hartman springs to mind – makes him a useful exemplar of what is right and wrong with deconstruction.

The problem of reference troubled him in his earlier book, *Blindness and Insight*, where he remarks: 'It would be quite foolish to assume that one can lightheartedly move away from the constraint of referential meaning.'[4] That de Man can consider the prospect shows how far things had gone, even in 1971 – not to speak of the fact that he thinks of reference as a constraint, not as the writer's objective. On the other hand, de Man is aware that the discrediting of crude referential theories (simple equivalences of words and things) has given undue licence to those who want to assert that language makes no reference at all. In *Allegories of Reading* he concedes that the fictionality and self-referentiality of literature are properties 'now perhaps somewhat too easily taken for granted',[5] remarking on 'the need to safeguard oneself from what might become a dangerous vertige, a dizziness of the mind caught in an infinite regress'.[6]

Such a vertige is what many deconstructors want for Christmas: they hail it in the titles of their books. And de Man too savours its joys when he discovers, or thinks he discovers, a rhetoric which 'suspends logic and opens up vertiginous possibilities of referential aberration'.[7] Scandal, danger, aberration, infinity, dizziness are common terms in deconstructive circles where a curious sensationalism prevails among hard-working professors whose idea of risk is the cocking of Nietzschean snooks at their own intellectual inheritance without the tiresome Nietzschean obligation to go out into the wilderness (though they *have* banished criticism there, as the title of one famous book proclaims[8]). They are also a reminder of existentialism's abiding influence and its vocabulary of predicament, menace and hazard. This is part of de Man's own background. Sartre's alien, unfathomable world becomes de Man's unreadable text. In both we are permanently stationed on the edge of an abyss between knowledge and reality. De Man describes this abyss in terms of the fraught yet necessary relationship between reference (to the real) and rhetoric (the form in which we are compelled to make that reference, and thus in which we have knowledge of it). Another of de Man's intellectual inheritances – from the New Critics – tells him that a literary text is, *par excellence*, a rhetorical construct with internal laws of its own governing (for example) the use of metaphors or the deployment of irony. At the same time it seems to make reference outside itself to a world with a different legal system. Yet we cannot know the one (the world) without the other (rhetoric – the name de Man gives to figures of speech). The two can never be made to coincide because no description is ever exhaustive and because language's relationship to the world is, anyway, uncertain. Yet each is unimaginable without the other: however surrealistically, language always refers to some extent; but however plain, it is also to some extent always metaphorical. Every utterance is both a rhetorical and a referential structure. We cannot separate the two, any more than we can separate the two sides of a piece of paper, but nor can we see them both at once. It is in this sense that literature is unreadable.

De Man argues his case in an opaque, muscle-bound style which symbolizes his struggle (in true existentialist fashion) with these difficult ideas. His problems begin when he tries to elaborate on their critical utility with reference to appropriate texts by Rousseau, Proust, Nietzsche and Rilke. Even the selection of authors (here and elsewhere) is suggestive of his standpoint. They are classics of modernism and pre-modernism, pillars of the alternative tradition so important to RLT. All indisputably first rank, they are nevertheless subtle, recondite, elusive and – most importantly – all preoccupied with the inner life, subordinating the external world to a profound exploration of spiritual and mental life. It is also striking that all four reflect obsessively on the uncertain relationship between the external world and their grasp of it. They are thus well suited to de Man's theory. Moreover, such material allows him to assume a good deal of what he needs to prove about his thesis.[9] How would Chaucer, Dryden or even Tolstoy bear out de Man's claim that language is duplicitous, literature unreadable, and reference always uncertain?

But even de Man's chosen authors do not always rest easy in his theoretical embrace. Take, for example, his remarks on a passage from Proust,[10] mentioned both in the introduction to *Allegories of Reading* and in a chapter on that writer. The passage is a characteristically Proustian meditation in which the writer, reading a book in the cool of his darkened room while the sun shines outside, reflects on the superiority of memory and imagination over experience. Direct contact with the sun could not possibly give him the full sense of summer he derives from the hints which reach him: buzzing flies, hammer blows outside the window, muted light, and so on. While de Man is right to bring out the subtleties of the experience described, it is easy to relate it to the book's announced theme, the search for past time. The narrator habitually discovers that experience takes on meaning only at several removes: his experience in the bedroom is a spatial equivalent for the temporal form of memory. He always needs, as it were, to stand at a distance from experience in order to savour it.

This is not how de Man reads Proust. He would view such an account as naïvely mimetic because he takes the view – common in certain kinds of RLT – that literature is not about the world but about itself. Thus his analysis of this passage concludes that while Proust thinks he is writing '*about* [his italics] the aesthetic superiority of metaphor over metonymy',[11] he is in fact demonstrating the reverse. As Christopher Butler has shown,[12] de Man's metaphor/metonymy distinction rests on dubious grounds, but that is not my point here. What concerns me is the assumption that literary texts are primarily self-referential. Literature on this view is 'about' its own rhetorical devices – though not in the sense that it discusses them explicitly, or even that it exemplifies them. On the contrary, de Man believes the reverse is true. As he puts it at the beginning of his book: 'The question is precisely whether a literary text is about that which it describes, represents or states.'[13] His answer is a resounding NO. Not only is a text *not* about what it describes, represents or states: it isn't even about the ways in which it does so, in the sense that *Tristram Shandy*, for example, directs our attention to novelistic techniques as much as to the content of its narrative. Literature is 'about' hidden processes, unknown even to (some would say 'especially to') the author. This is what makes criticism – and highly sophisticated criticism at that – so necessary. The critic isn't there simply to guide our attention to certain interesting features or to suggest ways of approaching a text. His role is to tell us what and how we think, and what the author was really aware of though he didn't know it.

This hubristic notion of the critic's role is made possible by the double movement of deconstruction. First it diverts attention from reference to difference – from the text's relationship with the world to its relationship with other texts and with itself. This immediately constitutes the critic as an expert. But then emphasis is moved again from the text to the reader. This might seem to confer freedom on readers – and in some way-out forms of deconstruction it does so – but only if we believe (and de Man doesn't) that reading is a subjective activity. On the contrary, it is an activity governed by complex rules – the rules embodied in rhetorical forms – and only the critic has a ready key to those rules, which require mastery of a high order.

The double movement from reference to difference, from the text to the reader, is made possible because deconstruction is a form of idealism which seems especially suited to the treatment of literature. *Books* may be things, but *texts* are structures of meaning whose hold on material existence, via the signs in which they are embodied, is tenuous. Given this point, de Man's strategic shifting of the literary emphasis from writing to reading is crucial. Bourgeois criticism thinks of the text as a product of the writer's experience. RLT thinks of the text as the product of the reader's activity. The writer is inescapably involved in the world of things at every level, from the activity itself – his attitude to the text as embodied in a book, something he has made – to the contents of the activity. Whatever radical theorists may say, most writers still think of themselves as writing about something which is not literature itself. Readers are in a rather different situation. They may relate a text to the world outside it, or they may not. Their activity is productive only in a mental, not a material sense. One could elaborate this distinction further, but the point about it is simple and crucial. The shift of critical attention from writing to reading is a shift of emphasis from reference to difference *before the discussion of texts even begins*. When this is supported, as it is in de Man, by a focus on writers whose theme is self-consciousness – and who are therefore their own readers – and who have a particular interest in the activities of writing and reading, the dice are loaded indeed.

Proust is an especially interesting case in this context because he belongs to the great tradition of French realism, and his perceptive criticisms of that tradition can only be understood in terms of his own part in it. *A la recherche du temps perdu* is, among other things, the greatest *roman fleuve* whose purpose is to underscore the ironic distance between the world we experience and what we make of it – an irony of which we can only become conscious if we believe – as Proust did – that this world can be apprehended and portrayed in literature. To make this point is not, of course, to contradict de Man's account of the complex relation between reference and rhetoric – but it is to throw doubt on his foregrounding of that relation. Putting the question at its crudest: if writers and readers over more than two millennia have overwhelmingly subscribed to the belief that literature is about the world first and itself second (and when that includes many of the writers de Man discusses), why should we believe otherwise? There is no question of proof either way. Criticism is no more a technology than literature is a science. We are not dealing here with questions of whether the sun moves round the earth, but with what people want and have wanted: a poetry which interprets their experience, not itself. To think otherwise is to mistake criticism's instruments for its substance.

Ever since the New Critics tried to deal with the Intentionalist Fallacy, the problem of reference has given most trouble not à propos the representation of the material world – an issue as old as Plato – but in terms of writerly intention. We can reformulate de Man's question in these terms:

> Whether or not a text is about what it describes, represents or states, does it do what its author says or thinks it does? How can we know? And does this matter?

New Criticism dismissed intention as unimportant, directing our attention to what the text – not the author – says and does. The application of biography to textual interpretation was especially frowned on by New Critics, who preferred exegesis to history. This didn't prevent the vast majority of readers (and critics) from talking about 'what the author means', from judging books in terms of their ability to fulfil avowed or apparent intentions, and from continuing to speculate on the relationship between how writers live and what they produce; but it did encourage the structuralist elimination of intention from literary criticism, and the deconstructive analysis of it as just one more part of the 'text'. New Critics, structuralists and their heirs want to say that intention is either irrelevant (because the text's meaning is determined by its rhetoric) or relevant only as an articulation of that rhetoric, not as something with a life of its own. Deconstructors want to say that intention is knowable only insofar as it is explicated in an interpretation of the text. Either way, the author vanishes. 'Authority' is quite literally invested in the text or in the reading of that text. What the poet feels about the death of his cat may be all very interesting but it can logically be the critic's concern only insofar as it is part of the poem, not as an expression of something 'outside' the poem.

The curious thing is that this academic nonsense increased in intensity proportionately with the popularity of exactly the opposite view among members of the reading public. Literary biography is a boom industry in our time, in print and on television. It seems that outside the academy, we can't get enough of 'what the author meant'. Perhaps this enthronement of the Author in popular esteem encouraged his assassination at the hands of theorists. Ironically, it has played its own part in forming the reputation of several theorists themselves. Where would Barthes the text be without Barthes the man? Elizabeth Bruss[14] has suggested that his theory is as much aesthetic spectacle as the texts he discusses – perhaps more so. A major aspect of this spectacle – what gives it meaning – is the biographical record it constitutes.

As if to recognize this point, RLT has now reinstated biography, in the form of yet another text, thus hoping to short-circuit the difficulty of accounting for the origins of discourse in real, historical subjects, without conceding that these beings are in any sense autonomous, or that their meaning in any way belongs to them or has its origins in their intentions. It is as though one were to say that the writer of a poison-pen letter had no responsibility for his work, or as though literary theorists were to forgo any royalties on their books on the grounds that it is language, not the author, who speaks. Thus Derrida can cheekily claim that 'the new status for us to discover is that of the relationship between life and text, between these two forms of textuality and the general writing in the play of which they are inscribed',[15] for all the world as if no one had ever considered the question before. Why we should need to discover the status of something Derrida has already decided to be a form of textuality is hard to say. Would it make this passage any less banal were we to substitute 'reality' for 'textuality', and 'existence' for 'general writing'? I suppose not.

Deconstructive critics are fond of 'inscribing' familiar issues in new jargon as though they were new problems for whose discovery the critic could claim credit while at the same time revealing the intellectual shallowness of bourgeois critics. Barthes, Derrida and de Man also have a trick of implying that if they had the time they would solve these new problems with a new form of logic or vocabulary previously unheard of. Take, for example, de Man's formulation of intentionalism.[16]

Referring once more to the passage from Proust, de Man alludes to the paragraph in which Marcel lies on his bed reading an adventure story. He takes this paragraph in context to suggest the pleasurable guilt with which Marcel for a moment unites 'fiction and action'. Reading is associated in the novel with the forbidden pleasures of daydreaming and masturbation: the moral world is the world of virile outdoor action as described in the adventure story which stirs Marcel. By reading this story, he can indulge his weakness by vicariously participating in an active life, freed for a while from his otherwise constant 'oscillation . . . between guilt and well-being'.

I don't suppose many people would disagree with de Man's account of the passage up to this point. But then, despite the assurance that his interpretation 'uses only the linguistic elements provided by the text itself' (whatever they may be), de Man begins to go seriously wrong, so eager is he to exclude from discussion all 'naïve questions' of reference, such as: Does Marcel know that he is combining guilt and well-being? Does Proust *know* it for him? These questions are 'absurd', says de Man, because 'the reconciliation of fact and fiction occurs itself as a mere assertion in the text'.[17] Now to begin with, there is no such assertion, only Marcel's comparison of the relations between the coolness of his room and the heat of the street outside; his repose and the excitement of the story he is reading; and a motionless hand in the middle of a running brook. In each case the one withstands *and* suggests the other. It is the contrast which makes each pair significant. And in each case, it is from the security of the first that Marcel can appreciate the second. In other words, the reconciliation of fact and fiction is what he does *not* assert: he hints at their reciprocal need as meaningful terms by underlining the contrast between them in three ways.

But even if there were such an assertion, naïve questions about the narrator's intention here are not only appropriate: they are a fundamental part of the writer's declared strategy. The whole point of this novel is that it works up to a moment of supreme insight near the end of the narrative which occurs late in the narrator's life. He determines to write his story in the light of this moment in order to show how it came about and how it required the whole of what appeared to be a wasted life in order to produce it. One may, of course, deny the validity of this moment from outside the text – calling it a delusion, for example, or a tragic mistake – but inside the text it is what the narrator uses to make sense of the whole narrative. In this context, the episode quoted by de Man appears as one of a series of incidents in which the narrator mistook his vocation – which is, of course, to become a writer: one for whom literature is the means of action. Marcel does not reveal this at the beginning of the book but he does know it, and it informs the structure of the entire story.

Thus the question of the narrator's motives at this point – though we can understand them only in the context of the whole book – is neither naïve nor absurd. By asserting that it is, de Man ignores the declared meaning of the novel. He is able to do this by appealing to a higher authority: his own reading of the text. This is not an unusual practice in any critical school, of course: perhaps every experienced reader secretly feels that he knows what a book means better than anyone else, including the author. But recent deconstructive and psychoanalytic approaches and the RLT which derives from them have given themselves warranty for every kind of outrageous interpretation by giving the text priority over the author. This has two consequences. First, it simply transfers the problem of intention from author to text: de Man's ingenuous claim that his reading uses only 'the linguistic elements provided by the text' is a way of sliding over this by pretending to critical neutrality while attributing all sorts of devious manoeuvres to the text (which is significantly put into the active tense). Secondly, the same form of words (linguistic elements etc.) neatly transfers to the critic the authority once attributed to the author and now nominally bestowed on the text. 'Proust doesn't know what he's doing, but I can tell you what the text is doing.' This is what de Man's critical practice amounts to: a fetishizing of textuality characteristic of all forms of deconstruction. There is little to choose between this and – say – Leavis's fetishizing of the author: both are masks for the dictatorship of the critic.

De Man's fetish leads him into much the same kinds of trouble as Leavis's. Both writers are marked by a distinctive combination of sophistication and arbitrariness. There is no need to read further than Chapter 1 in *Allegories of Reading* to see that. Take, for example, de Man's remarks about truth – evidently a topic close to his heart. In the midst of many telling comments on the passage from Proust discussed above, he makes some truly astonishing claims – astonishing, that is, in the light of his theoretical stance. De Man thinks that poets are sources of truth and that critic-philosophers, i.e., deconstructive critics, are their prophets – though the prophets are rendered redundant by de Man's assertion, in passing, that literary texts are anyway the best examples of self-deconstruction. Be that as it may, he insists on the truth-claim, defining it perplexingly as 'the recognition of the systematic character of a certain kind of error'.[18] De Man does not make it clear what this error is, but we may suppose that it is the kind into which we are led by rhetoric. Truth and error need one another. Truth (or at least poetic truth) is therefore always negative.

I don't claim to understand this point – and I have serious reservations about the deconstructive habit of turning criticism into pseudo-philosophy – but I do know that on the very same page de Man blithely uses both 'true' and 'false' in an absolute and not a relative sense. He tells us that certain claims about Proust's texts are 'not true' and that the conventional writer/reader distinction is 'false' – a point his own reading makes 'evident'. Even more surprisingly, he goes on to say that this reading is 'not "our" reading, since it uses only the linguistic elements provided by the text itself . . . it is not something we have added to the text, but it constituted the text in the first place'.[19] This is pretty breathtaking critical hubris by any standards. It also goes clean against two planks of de Man's own theory: (1) that literature is duplicitous and unreadable; and (2) that the critic always rewrites the text in his own image. But these points are already contradictory: if true, they make de Man's own text unintelligible. The only way out of this paradox is to assume that we can in fact 'know' the text in ways we cannot know reality outside it.

Needless to say, the text is not the only thing de Man 'knows' in practice. His knowledge turns out to reach quite beyond normal human powers. Discussing Derrida's critique of Rousseau, for example, de Man assures us that Derrida 'had to go out of his way' not to understand Rousseau,[20] implying that he, de Man, understands Rousseau well enough to know how and why Derrida does not. He even knows things about Rousseau which Rousseau didn't know, although he derives his knowledge from Rousseau's own testimony. So much is clear from his commentary on the famous passage from Rousseau's *Confessions* in which the autobiographer explains at length his reasons for letting a servant girl take responsibility for the theft of a ribbon stolen by Rousseau himself. This has become something of a *locus classicus* for the intentional controversy because of the evident complexity of its author's motives. Jean-Jacques twists and turns round the problem of his guilt, unwilling to admit it, yet apparently compelled by remorse to go over the episode again and again, even to the extent of recording it twice, here and in the fourth *Reverie*.

De Man first explains that the ribbon is really a substitute for Marion (the maid) as the object of Rousseau's desire. The passage is therefore about his desire. But de Man then doubles back to the conflict between unacknowledgeable guilt and true remorse to conclude that 'what Rousseau *really* [his italics] wanted was neither the ribbon nor Marion, but the public scene of exposure which he actually gets'.[21] This analysis is surprising for a number of reasons. First, because it sets up the notion of Rousseau's desire for Marion at the cost of considerable critical manipulation of the text, only to pull it down again in favour of another desire (for exposure). But why should de Man take Rousseau through the (hypothetical) detour of his desire for Marion when the exposure-conclusion can be reached more easily by direct appeal to the existence of two texts, which points to Rousseau's compulsive need to confess? Putting aside a taste for gratuitous complexity (not an inconsiderable motive, given the sheer momentum of the deconstructive machine) it seems to be the result of de Man's need to extract a full and coherent account of Rousseau's behaviour from the text itself, without reference to the historical figure of Rousseau, which would so seriously compromise his textualism. As we shall see in the following chapter, history is an embarrassment for textualists because – *pace* Derrida – its own status as a text is not easy to fathom, and it reintroduces the problem of reference in a particularly trying way.

As it happens, I suspect de Man is right about the historical Rousseau who represents himself in this text. His relish for self-exposure and self-punishment (at the hands of others) is well documented in the *Confessions* and elsewhere – which makes it all the sillier for de Man to produce this conclusion so triumphantly out of his rhetorical hat, when it is there for all to see. But why should de Man suppose that this is an exclusive desire? Rousseau himself claims not to know why he behaved as he did. Perhaps he wanted the ribbon 'then' and the scene of exposure 'now', as he reflects on the events later. We don't know – and that is the point. It is absurd of de Man to pronounce the unreadability of the text in the same breath as he claims certainty (what Rousseau *really* wanted) about what we can learn from it. And by what justice in the world can he conclude that 'Marion was destroyed . . . to furnish him with a good ending for Book II of his *Confessions*'?[22]

This is rhetoric without reference with a vengeance. Even fantastic hyperbole is brought in to thematize a reading of the text in what amounts to a parody of New Criticism, where every detail is bent in conformity to the determining and unifying principle which informs the critical exegesis and, by implication, the text itself. It is precisely this principle, of course, which an older tradition of bourgeois criticism is said to derive from the intention of the author, and which a newer tradition of pragmatic criticism proposes to constitute as the author's intention (in the sense that intention and meaning are simply the same thing). The curious point about de Man's recourse to a reading of the text where everything fits (including the things that don't appear to do so at first glance) is that deconstruction, by his own testimony, is meant to show us that there are no determining or unifying principles, no certain knowledge, no 'reallys'.

It is no more unreasonable for de Man to cleave to New Critical unitarianism than it is for him to keep faith with phenomenological intentionalism. The problem is to reconcile these with deconstructive scepticism and a methodology characterized by Barbara Johnson as the teasing out of warring forces.[23] Indeed, looked at in this way, deconstruction is simply one logical outcome of the New Critical interest in irony, ambiguity and paradox, with the unifying context removed. As such, deconstruction is already implicit in the work of a critic such as William Empson. Its development is prevented only by the invocation of context, use or common sense. But de Man's drive towards a pure textualism leaves these restraints behind, while not abandoning the referential criteria which give rise to them. Thus his approach to Rousseau depends not only on a notion of textual unity, but also on an implicit psychical and biographical unity 'behind' or 'in' the text. Given the de Manic principle of critical blindness, however, we find ourselves in the paradox that this unity could not be known to Rousseau himself, only revealed to us. The critic is thus privileged to know more about the unknowable subject than the subject itself because he (the critic) knows the text – or, as de Man might put it, the text knows him.

The point is confirmed by two commentators on de Man's account of Rousseau which, according to Christopher Norris, is 'not, of course, the kind of intentionalist reading which the old New Critics – and the Stucturalists after them – so firmly rejected. Without wishing to claim that Rousseau intended, or consciously grasped any such latent possibilities of meaning, de Man puts the case that his texts in themselves provide the only starting point for deconstructive treatment.'[24] Is Norris being ingenuous when he implies that other sorts of criticism do not take texts as their starting-point? And what, I wonder, does he mean by 'texts in themselves'[25] – a phrase which comes close to the New Critical formula of the 'words on the page'? If textuality is radically uncontrollable, a point of intersection for many modes and codes, how can there be such a thing as the text in itself?

In the last chapter I commented on the difficulty structuralists had when trying to work out what a literary object is. Here we confront the same problem seen from the deconstructive point of view. Just what is a text? How is it to be distinguished from the non-textual? The extreme solution to these problems – that everything is textual, that there is nothing outside the text – has proved more popular than coherent, and most critics (de Man and Norris included) settle in practice for the softer option of quietly assuming the traditional distinction between the textual and the non-textual, the differential and the referential. Only thus could Norris tell us (continuing the quotation above) that de Man 'goes to quite remarkable lengths to demonstrate the gap between Rousseau's apparent topics of discourse . . . and the textual dynamics that govern and . . . undermine them'.[26] For otherwise how could Norris attribute topics to Rousseau at all – whether as a real or as a rhetorical figure? Or perhaps topics are rhetorical figures too. Or is the idea of a rhetorical figure itself a rhetorical figure? And how could he distinguish between 'apparent' topics and presumably 'real' textual dynamics, except by reference to something outside the text – say, a notion of what might constitute textual dynamics?

The trouble with this sort of analysis is its presupposition that the text has a reality denied to the non-text (and whatever Derrida may say about there being 'nothing outside the text', presumably even deconstructors have some notion of the non-textual: if not, what meaning can the concept 'text' possibly have?).

William Ray, commenting on the same passage in de Man, tries to be more precise. He, too, wants to rescue de Man from the horrors of reference and intention, and he proposes to do so via speech-act theory. The vital task is to get rid of Rousseau the historical person and origin of the *Confessions*, so that we can read Rousseau the text in peace and quiet. How do we achieve this?

> If one can show the efficacy of linguistic performatives to be a function of their independence from acts of personal will, the 'initiation' and the 'conclusion' of critical reading will no longer appear the result of authorial intention.[27]

By the time Ray appears on the critical scene, of course, there is no need to explain to a sophisticated audience why in the world one should *want* to escape from the horrors of authorial intention: that can be safely assumed. The important thing is simply to isolate the text from its origins, and to allow it to 'assume responsibility for meaning'.[28]

But once the text is firmly sealed off from any external reality, it won't have any meaning: there will be nothing for it to mean. The fact is that the text doesn't 'assume responsibility' for anything: that is simply transferred from writer to reader. And reference doesn't disappear, it is relocated from the relation between text and world to the relation between text and readerly consciousness.

De Man employs the same tactic, telling us that 'as soon as a text knows what it states, it can only act deceptively ... and if a text does not act, it cannot state what it knows'.[29] But in what possible sense can a text know or act? And if it is the text and not the writer or the reader who knows, how can de Man know whether it acts or knows, deceptively or otherwise? Ever more curiously, what are we to make of the phrase 'as soon as' here? Are we to suppose that in the temporal activity which reading involves it is the text which undergoes variation and not the reader? Is the text somehow alive? It certainly seems to have acquired an intention and a pathos now denied to the writer. How ironic that radical literary theory should rescue us from the romantic urge to exalt the author, only to replace him with the text.

This is what happens in Barbara Johnson's brief essay 'Teaching Deconstructively' when she insists that 'Teaching literature is teaching how to read ... what the language is doing, not guess what the author was thinking',[30] as though language and thought, authors and texts, had nothing to do with one another. But it is, of course, precisely the activities of reading and writing which unite these things. Johnson's rhetorical oppositions – language and author, doing and thinking, reading and guessing – are factitious. Writers and readers are people who use language. Texts come from somewhere and go somewhere: they have a function, or many functions. In reading and writing, thinking is doing. And while Johnson is correct in her assertion that a text can signify

'somethng more, something less, or something other than it
claims to',[31] this assertion itself would be meaningless without
a standard by which to measure what more, less and other
are. Intention is one way of deriving this standard but it is
not the only way. We may, for example, compare what a text
does – say, a sonnet – with what we know of other instances
in the genre; with other similar texts by the same writer; with
other texts on a similar theme or using similar language; and
so on. The error is to make intention an either/or matter
(either all texts intend or none do) and to assume that every
text – everything made out of words – must have the same
intentional status. In some cases, 'what the author was
thinking' and 'what the language is doing' effectively coincide
for all interpretive purposes. In others they do not. Either
way, only the context can decide, and the context is not
simply a matter of readerly choice (as the later Barthes is
inclined to assume) or what the language determines (as de
Man and Johnson think), but of cultural assumptions and
hermeneutic practices too complex ever to be fully specified.
Which is not to say that we should not try to specify them,
only that such specification will always inevitably be crudely
approximate, and that the minuscule linguistic distinctions of
deconstruction are, in the end, self-defeating. Excessive
interpretive minuteness may lead to hermeneutic infinity but
it ends in a critical blind alley.

Johnson more or less concedes this in her brilliant essay
'The Frame of Reference' (reprinted in *The Critical Difference*) in which biographical criticism makes a casual re-entry.
In pursuit of the theme that all reading is misreading, that
there is no correct interpretation, that the critic reproduces
the text in his own image, Johnson explores Lacan's account
of Poe's story 'The Purloined Letter' and Derrida's critique of
Lacan's account, making the personal antagonism between
the two men a central feature of her discussion. Both Lacan
and Derrida have something at stake in their very different
interpretations of Poe's narrative. The story of their readings

therefore becomes in part the story of their lives – of their own critical blindnesses. Each reads himself into the text – or as de Man would say, allegorizes it. There is no univocal meaning: to read is therefore to engage in unconscious autobiography, and Johnson concludes her essay by inviting the reader to locate the blindnesses which appear in her account of Poe, Lacan and Derrida.

One curious result of this approach is to make all texts autobiographical, which is true but trivially so. The point of criticism is not to make vague generalizations but useful distinctions. All text is autobiographical, i.e., self-revealing, to the same extent that all autobiography is fictional, i.e., self-concealing. This is not a very interesting observation. What matters are the differences between those texts which intend autobiography and those which do not. Only in the light of such declared intention do these generalizations become interesting. In other words, intention is a crucial factor in the case of autobiography or texts we want to regard as autobiographical, where it must be presumed.

We can approach this problem another way by asking what Johnson means when she says that every text 'stages the modes of its own misreadings'?[32] Presumably this does not simply imply that any text can be made to mean anything, but relates only to responsible interpretations, i.e., those which result from genuine attempts (intentions) to arrive at a meaning. But taking good faith for granted, does that mean that every misreading is of equal value – that my misreading of Mallarmé and Johnson's have the same merit? And is there no difference between misreading and misunderstanding? If so, how are we to recognize it? How, in short, are we to know 'what the language is doing' and what it is not doing? If no approximation to correct interpretation is possible, how can it be said to be 'doing' anything remotely verifiable?

The point here is that Lacan, Derrida and Johnson all give different accounts of 'The Purloined Letter' but these accounts come within a relatively narrow range determined by a number of contexts (of which intention could be one, though they do not postulate it as such). And it is of course context which determines what counts as biography and what as fiction; what counts as a good misreading and what as a bad one; what the difference is between intention and achievement. And if it is true, as Derrida has observed, that every context has a context, or as Johnson would put it, that every frame can itself become a picture and every picture a frame, it is also true, as Wittgenstein remarked, that reasons must stop somewhere. In her essay on 'Teaching Deconstructively' Johnson contrasts deconstruction as 'a reading strategy that carefully follows both the meanings and the suspensions and displacements of meaning in a text, while humanism is a strategy to stop reading when the text stops saying what it ought to have said',[33] but once again her opposition is factitious. Every type of reading stops at this point. The difference between deconstruction and 'humanism' (assuming that Johnson means by this word what Barthes means by bourgeois criticism) is no greater than the differences between critics within these two approaches. Both have their virtues, but on the debit side there is no difference between dogmatic positivism and dogmatic scepticism. Reasons must stop somewhere. Where they stop depends not on the establishment of ultimate metaphysical grounds (which Derrida and Johnson believe cannot be found) but on the conventions of practice which – as Johnson must very well know – includes consideration of the 'suspensions and displacements of meaning in a text' as frequently in 'humanism' as it does in deconstruction. Or did Empson live in vain?

But perhaps Empson and Wittgenstein are not suitable authorities to quote against deconstruction's irrationalism, whose whole purpose is to push critical analysis, not only beyond the borders of the reasonable, and beyond all the commonly recognized and conventionally functional distinctions between its own concepts – but beyond the very disciplinary distinctions which traditionally constitute criticism as an activity. As Johnson puts it, literature makes visible the 'literarity' even at 'the heart of theory'. Structuralism encouraged us to make criticism more theoretical. Deconstruction discovers that theory is just more literature. Indeed, it seems that every kind of writing is literature, there is nothing but literature. When, as de Man puts it, 'literature is everywhere; what they call anthropology, linguistics, psychoanalysis, is really nothing but literature',[34] one may as well abandon talk of reasons and contexts altogether. The 'they' in this quotation refers to 'modern critics who think they are demystifying literature' (structuralists and Marxists) when 'they are in fact being demystified by it'.

If it were true that everything turns into literature, this would be gloomy news indeed for the critic. When everyone is somebody, no one's anybody. If everything is literature, nothing is, and the literary critic as such is out of a job. But this is not quite the situation. De Man has got his formula the wrong way round. The problem for criticism is not that everything turns into literature but that literature turns into everything. From Plato onwards discussions about literature have invariably tended to turn into discussions about something else: politics, philosophy, anthropology, psychology, history, even physiology and geography.

This has two interesting implications. First, that far from being non-referential, as certain extreme textualists want to claim, literature is by definition meaningful: it always points to something other than itself. This is why structuralism and deconstruction fail to the extent that they claim to be purely technical accounts of the 'literary' and succeed to the extent that their practice (as opposed to their theory) takes account of reference.

The second implication concerns the function of literary pedagogy. Commenting on the tendency of critical discussions to become discussions of the non-literary, Barbara Johnson concludes from this that the teacher should confine herself to teaching reading – in the phrase cited earlier: 'how to read what the language is doing, not guess what the author was thinking'.[35] But as I have suggested – and as de Man's own theory implies – these two cannot be separated: coming to grips with the topic of a text is part of learning how to read it. The study of literature cannot simply be reduced to rhetorical analysis, however important a part this plays. Insofar as the study of literature is the study of reading – and I shall have something to say about this in my last chapter – it must take account of what is read. The best deconstruction – including some of Johnson's own – does this. But for the most part it claims to be concentrating on the 'how'.

We have seen the problems with this approach: it is now time to consider the problems of critical theories which concentrate on the 'what' – and for RLT the 'what' invariably means ideology.

5

Memories and Reflections

> His theory, insofar as I can understand it,
> seems to discount the testimony of human
> experience . . .

Thus far we have considered examples from two radical
theoretical modes — structuralism and deconstruction — in
which supposedly conventional notions of the relationships
between world and writer, writer and text, text and reader,
reader and critic, have been challenged. The notions that
literature represents reality, that it expresses something the
writer has to communicate, and that this something can be
understood by the reader, are all at best rendered problematic, at worst dismissed as fantastic. The structure of the text
takes the place of the book, meaning is controlled not by
human subjects but by language, its grammar and tropes; and
reality becomes their projection. Art, on this view, is not
merely the model for Nature but its origin and horizon.

All these challenges to received opinion are salutary,
though invariably overdeveloped. The angry rejection of
'common sense', equated with the belief that we do have
some immediate access to reality not finally determined by
the structure of language (itself supposed to be immediately
accessible in ways denied to the external world), tends to
stand between theorists and the perception of their own
theoretical inconsistencies. This hardly matters when we are
concerned only with the aesthetic pleasure to be derived from
the completeness or newness of the theory itself. It does
matter when we consider the practical implications for criticism. For the critic changes with the theory. His traditional

tasks of description, evaluation and interpretation, all supposed to mediate between text and reader, become meaningless. His activities are emptied of content, becoming merely formal. He is seen as a master-semiologist or rhetorician whose positive cultural and social functions give way to negative dialectic: he is reduced to revealing the true meaning behind verbal appearances (structuralism) or to showing that there are no such things as truth and meaning except in the most fleeting sense.

In practice, of course, there is more to structuralism and deconstruction than this: they frequently have a political or ethical content and a didactic design on the reader, who is led to concur in this or that view by his assent to this or that methodology. The connection between epistemological radicalism and radical politics here, however, is rhetorical: there is no necessary link between the two, as will be apparent from the foregoing discussions of Barthes and de Man. The undermining of conventional critical attitudes, or even of humanistic categories of understanding (insofar as that is what such writers provide) is not, of itself, politically subversive, though it often appears to be so. My choice of major examples was partly dictated by the need to make this point. Indeed, writers on the far left often comment suspiciously on the political credentials of literary theorists – especially deconstructors – who are seen to cultivate a version of Nietzschean, i.e., right-wing, scepticism. For if there is no end to interpretation, if all values are in a permanent state of revaluation, if there is nothing 'outside' the text – then political action appears to become meaningless, just another gesture in the endless proliferation of textuality. And if that is the case, not only is there no necessary link between radical theory and radical politics: radical theory is itself just another text, another gesture, on a level of equality with all the supposed errors of liberal humanism. There is no better and worse, there is only different. What is more, theory remains what it has always been: a marginal activity of no general interest or political significance.

This is where Marxism comes into the theoretical story, for these are the weaknesses Marxism hopes to confront and correct, and it has recently tried to do so by salvaging what it can from those very structuralist and deconstructive theories to which it is in some respects most bitterly opposed. For as Hayden White has put it, 'The best reasons for being a Marxist are moral ones'[1] – and such a prior ethical commitment is anathema to all forms of theoretical scepticism. In consequence, it is within Marxism that we find the crucial battles and *rapprochements* between radical theory and revolutionary politics which give rise to RLT conceived as a major political weapon. Marxism, in other words, restores the social and cultural functions of criticism but only by revealing them as ultimately political. The critic as decoder (structuralism) and the critic as interpreter (deconstruction) are superseded by the critic as activist.

There is a certain irony here, insofar as Marxism is the heir of those very liberal traditions that radical theorists denounce, and the comparisons are illuminating. Like Christianity, which forms the ideological basis of Western liberal societies, Marxism is founded not on scientific predictions but on the metaphysical sanction of a millennial vision. This vision underwrites the moral commitment to which White refers. Marxism is thus a theology as well as a theory. The decline of metaphysical authority has therefore proved as troublesome for Marxists as for Christians, and in similar ways, fragmenting them into rival sects and – more significantly – directing their attention away from the action necessary to attain a future heaven (whether in this world or the next) and towards arguments about a text (the Bible, the writings of Marx and Engels). Both Marxism and Christianity are moral philosophies inscribed in theologies of the word, and this doubleness has been their strength and their undoing. Incited to turn from contemplation to action by their leaders,

Christians and Marxists have made the very words in which this instruction is expressed a temptation to refrain from obeying it, detained from virtuous action by the imperative need for right interpretation.

Marx's Judaism would have made him well aware that Biblical exegesis is a dominant model for Western intellectual activity. The problem for revolutionary politics is how to transform such exegesis into the grounds for action – or, as Marx put it himself: philosophers have so far only interpreted the world, now their task is to change it. But this famous formula is not as clear as it seems, for the distinction between interpretation and action – between understanding something and altering it – is not a simple one. Indeed, there is a profound split at the very heart of Marx's own theory: between Marxism as a call to revolutionary action, and Marxism as a scientific description of social laws whose inevitable working cannot be altered by human participation. One might say much the same of Christianity, which confronts the believer with an uncomfortable choice between God's immutable laws of election and reprobation and the possibility of grace through good works. Protestantism inclines to the first, Catholicism to the second. In practice, both occupy an uneasy middle ground, on which God is the ultimate arbiter of all, but Man is left a little room for manoeuvre.

Much the same is true of most versions of Marxism, which replace God with the Economy while allowing human intervention in the political sphere to count for something. The problem for Marxist literary critics and theorists is to explain what that 'something' is in their case. Marx himself sensibly sidestepped the issue by treating literature as though it had nothing much to do with revolution: his profound knowledge and enjoyment of Shakespeare were founded on a trust in that writer's fidelity to notions of 'human nature' which latterday Marxists find scandalous. Nor are they amused by Engels's injunction to a committed writer: that it is more important to write a good novel than a socialist one. This lack of amusement has to do with a regard for their own role. Early Marxist criticism tends to fall into two types, the one evaluating works according to their ideological soundness, the other cataloguing them according to the ways in which they exemplify Marxist laws of historical and cultural evolution. The problem with both activities is that they are mere extensions of bourgeois criticism, replacing traditional value-judgments and historical explanations with the same thing in Marxist terms. They are thus compromised at a deep level by bourgeois ideology in the sense that they do nothing to bring about a revolutionary transformation of the institutions from which they derive: instead of abolishing the decadent power-structures of the academy (which constitute a major pillar of the bourgeois state and its instrument of ideological indoctrination) they merely fiddle around with its vocabulary. Their activities are thus not only marginal to the desired revolution: they can actually be counterproductive (unless, that is, one believes that strengthening the bourgeois state is a good thing because it intensifies the internal tensions of capitalism which will ultimately forward the collapse of bourgeois society).

This problem arises because traditional Marxist criticism is based on a variety of the reflection model, i.e., the view that works of art picture a reality external and prior to themselves, and that they are validated by accuracy of reference to that reality. But the reflection model is absolutely fundamental to bourgeois ideology whose whole enterprise, according to Marxism, is to persuade us that the world pictured in classical art is the real one, its class values (repression of a proletariat by a ruling class) forever insulated from change because that's just how things are. Bourgeois society thus uses art and a mimetic theory of art to shore up its own position. Marxist aesthetic theory simply adapted the reflection model to its own purposes, with very awkward results. For it was forced to conclude either that art merely reflects the prevailing social realities of the epoch, and is therefore of interest only as a social record (which is manifestly untrue); or that it reflects the underlying realities (i.e., the laws of social and economic evolution as revealed by Marxism), in which case it is often in violent and paradoxical conflict with its own avowed ideological position. Either way, a great deal of overingenious explanation is needed to account for the history of literature. More importantly, both theories make art a decorative activity of little interest to the serious revolutionary who, like Lenin, would like to listen to Beethoven if he could spare the time from more important matters, such as cutting off heads.

This leaves Marxist critics and theorists with a number of unpleasant dilemmas. For one thing, they are in danger of becoming apologists for bourgeois art. For another, is it not possible that art is somehow *intrinsically* bourgeois, the product of privileged leisure hours, a useless luxury, which will anyway be unnecessary after the revolution? And if art is superfluous, what is the use of criticism – not to speak of theory? What contribution can writers make to the revolution other than polemical pamphlets and inspiring poems? How is Marxist criticism to fulfil Marx's injunction – to get away from interpreting the past and join in changing the present? How is the critic to move from one side of Marxism – simply expounding the ineluctable laws of dialectical materialism – to the other: an active role in transforming society?

These questions have been rendered more urgent in recent years by Marxism's encounters with revolutionary movements within art: modernism and post-modernism. At first disdained on the left as sterile aestheticism, the last resort of decadent bourgeois society, the avant garde at last proved such a challenge to Marxist criticism that it had to be taken on. The alternatives were an increasingly hysterical trust in social realism of just the kind Marx and Engels deplored, and which produced a risible canon of unreadable novels; or moral gyrations of the Sartrean sort, necessary to explain how apparently anti-socialist modernist texts (Céline is the

119

most intriguing example) can be assimilated to a Marxist cultural scheme.

In short, if Marxist critics and theorists were to redeem their honour and find a vital political role, they had to do something about the reflection model. They had to show, first of all, that literature is not merely a copy of the world, either in appearance or reality. They then had to demonstrate that their own activities extended to more than interpretation, in the bourgeois sense, or to semiological and rhetorical analysis in the radical sense. What both demonstrations needed to amount to was proof that literature, criticism and theory all act on the world in some vital sense. At the same time they had to avoid falling into the liberal humanist trap of assuming that such action is 'moral' in the sense that it concerns the individual. A Marxist theory of criticism must not be a theory of personal experience, of infinitely variable readerly expectation and fulfilment. It must be a social theory, in the sense that it accounts for broad laws of historical evolution. But since the central task of criticism is always one form or another of exegesis, this will be a political theory of reading, i.e., a way of making interpretation the basis for – or even the form of – action.

The scriptural warranty for such a theory is to be found in the scattered remarks of Marx and Engels to the effect that literature is not valuable only as a record of social life, and that it is not merely a reflection of the economic base – except, in Engels's famous phrase, 'in the last resort'. Lukács[2] developed this view into the proposition that an author's avowed intentions do not necessarily correspond with the truth revealed by the text. Although Balzac was royalist, Catholic and conservative, his novels reveal the true state of affairs in Restoration France, where the monarchy, the church and the government were all rotten. And however much the novelist may proclaim his admiration for the adventuresses, cads and seedy aristocrats who people his work, they are shown, by the very force of Balzac's realism, for the dismal lot they are, trapped in their romantic illusions, and ripe for revolution.

Now there are plenty of legitimate objections to Lukács's account of Balzac, which perhaps tries too hard to fit this protean novelist into the straitjacket of a naïve historical theory. But the really interesting thing about such an account is not the objections to it but the problem it reveals. Lukács – himself steeped and educated in the most sophisticated traditions of middle European bourgeois culture – accepts the masterpieces of Western literature at their conventional (bourgeois) valuation. At the same time, he wants to find new (Marxist) grounds for that valuation, in order to preserve his literary heritage from the fate reserved by Marxism for bourgeois political, social and economic institutions. Hence his decision to separate Balzac's texts from the author's opinions. This also has the advantage of making texts the products of social laws, not individual acts of will. What Balzac wrote superficially reflects his own attitudes, but reveals at a deeper level the underlying structure of social reality.

This underlying structure is theorized by Lukács as the concept of ideology, defined by Marx as the ruling ideas in society, which are themselves no more than 'the ideal expression of the dominant material relationships grasped as ideas'.[3] In Lukács's influential variation on this formula, ideology is the unconscious body of ruling ideas, which can manifest themselves in literature in spite of authorial intentions. Hence the dual aspect of Balzac's fiction.

The concept of ideology has been crucial in Marxist attempts to get away from reflection theory and to accommodate the revolutionary implications of modernism. Often used as a pejorative term on all sides to describe the deluded beliefs of others, much as Plato contrasts opinion unfavourably with true knowledge, ideology has a more profound significance within Marxism. In particular, the ideological analysis of art has been seen as a way of bridging the gap between interpretation and action. This happens when the traditional formula is reversed as, for example, in the work of Gramsci. Marx and Lukács see ideology as the product of material relationships, but recent writers have suggested that it can condition those relationships, and even that ideological critique is an essential step towards revolutionary change. Where the superstructure (laws, culture etc.) was once thought to be determined by the economic base, it is now held that the two are mutually interactive.

Something of this sort can be found in the writings of Althusser, who takes the argument one step further by suggesting that ideology is not an optional extra, which would not exist in a truly Marxist society, but a condition of life. One writer has summarized it as 'the way men live the relation between themselves and their real conditions of existence',[4] while another, thinking of its relevance for the literary critic, has called it 'the imaginary ways in which men experience the real world'.[5] The difference between these summaries points to the difficulty of summarizing the hugely influential but obscure Althusser. Perhaps the combination of obscurity and influence says something about RLT. What the summaries share – as suggested by the word 'real' – is the view that ideology is not a tiresome bourgeois delusion to be swept away by rigorous Marxist analysis, but a fact of existence. It occupies the role assigned to belief in other philosophical systems: the inevitable preliminary to any dealings with the world. And like belief, its roots are by definition beyond complete explanation.

This does not mean that ideology/belief is beyond all explanation, however, and Althusser's bizarre 'science' is an attempt, influenced by structuralism, to devise a systematic method of revealing their workings. According to Althusser, what the scientist, i.e., the Marxist theoretician, studies is not reality (forever concealed from us by an ideological veil) but our interpretations of it, which are themselves manifestations of ideology. These interpretations he calls Generalities (1).

The scientist applies to them Generalities (2): the dialectical method of reasoning. He thereby arrives at 'knowledge': Generalities (3). The entire process is mental: at no point is reference made to a 'real' external world – which is rather curious in the context of a materialist philosophy. Indeed, Marx himself had already commented on such curiosity in *The German Ideology* where he witheringly remarks that 'Once upon a time an honest fellow had the idea that men were drowned in water only because they were possessed with the idea of gravity. If they were to knock this idea out of their heads, say, by stating it to be a superstition, a religious idea, they would be sublimely proof against any danger from water.'[6] The odd thing about this quotation is that it simultaneously provides Althusser with his premise – that ideology cannot simply be disposed of – while accurately anticipating the absurdity of his approach. Marx's ironic common sense undermines Althusser's project from the start. If the distinction between science and ideology is purely theoretical, what is the use of it? And how is it made in the first place, except by reference to our experience of an actual world?

Even more problematic is the distinction between science, which gives us knowledge of ideology, and art, which gives us the imaginative experience of it. In terms of this distinction literary criticism (or, at any rate, literary theory) is a form of science, a critique of the ideological formations to be found in literary texts. Stripped of the theoretical fol-de-rol, this sounds suspiciously like a conventional view of the literature/criticism relationship, and it is. Literature (ideology) gives us a complex illusion (interpretation) in problematic relation to the 'real'. The critic's (scientist's) task is to illuminate some of the complexities and problems. This appears to restore the critic to his traditional role as cultural commentator or even semiological guru, while reducing his specific political significance. However there are complications. To begin with, the definition already quoted which gives us ideology as 'the imaginary ways in which men experience the real world', while also giving us a definition of literature (as Terry Eagleton points out) only gives us part of the definition. For literary texts are said to have the distinctive quality of both reproducing the dominant ideology while at the same time making it explicit and thereby criticizing it through that very reproduction. (Indeed, this has been suggested as one method of accounting for value-judgments, in terms of the extent to which a text merely restates current assumptions and the extent to which it subjects them to investigation.) So literature is, in a sense, both ideology and science, both illusion and critique. (This is a common notion in twentieth-century theory – formalism, New Criticism, stucturalism.)

This of itself would hardly have important consequences for the critic, who could still profitably employ himself drawing attention to features of the text, were it not for the pessimistic Althusserian view that there is no escape from ideology. For if it is the product of our relations with the real, any change in those relations can only produce not truth in any objective sense, but a new ideological formation. Reality is a mental construct: there can be no ultimate knowledge of it. This leaves the critic in the peculiar situation of knowing that he does not know; of knowing that there is a distinction between science and ideology but being unable to say exactly what it is; of knowing that ideology is the way men live the relation with their real conditions of existence, but unable to say at any given time what those real relations are, because anything he says about them will be ideologically determined – and so on and so forth. In short, Althusser's Marxism arrives at the same point as de Man's deconstruction: a position which is both sceptical and dogmatic, in which empirical knowledge is 'rigorously' excluded, only to return in the ever more blatant form of theoretical pronouncements about reference, the Real etc. etc.

One can see this paradox at work in Eagleton's heroic struggle to make sense of Althusser for literary purposes in

Criticism and Ideology, where theoretical subtleties persistently give way to the writer's grosser critical convictions. Eagleton here expounds his usual historical scheme of bourgeois capitalism's decline through a sort of Leavisite parody in which he reviews Eng. Lit. between Arnold and Lawrence. Part of his design is to discredit realism, whether Leavisite or Lukácsian, by linking its evolution to the rise and fall of capitalist ideology. He tries to do this by showing how that ideology (which is, of course, the ideology of liberalism) actively strives to conceal its wicked origins in the material world and the repression of the proletariat. But for all its striving, bourgeois ideology cannot quite conceal the internal contradictions which will eventually tear it apart. These are manifested especially in the increasing sensationalism and violence of realistic literature on the one hand (a direct revelation of capitalist brutality of the sort chronicled by Leavis and Raymond Williams) and the self-deception of a retreat into the private world of love, spirituality, depth psychology and private experience, on the other (an indirect testimony to the pressures of monopoly capitalism, and at the same time an effort to conceal them).

Eagleton comments on a number of myths of this kind (the purest form of bourgeois ideology, as Barthes has taught us); the most important among them being the organic society, singling out the novelists of late Victorian England for their culpable complicity in such myths. A particular criminal is Henry James. Like John Goode (whom he quotes), Eagleton[7] sees James as a high priest of late capitalism, remote from reality, and unable to write about much more than silly heiresses who have 'so much money they no longer need to think about it'. He cites Isabel Archer and Milly Theale in support of this view – which is odd because both are distinguished by the passionate desire to make good use of their wealth. Isabel is in time enlightened but crushed by her burden, while Milly is betrayed. These are hardly tales of light-headed floozies quaffing champagne while proletarian children starve, but profoundly ironic tragi-comedies. In common with a number of other James stories – *In the Cage, The Princess Casamassima, The Bostonians* and others – they explore the encounter between poverty and wealth, both material and spiritual, and the relationship between the material conditions of men and their moral and social welfare. One could even describe *Portrait of a Lady* and *The Wings of the Dove* as Marxist fables in which the ambiguous and unseen power of capital and the contradictions it involves are vividly painted. James's interest in millionaires – Maggie and her father in *The Golden Bowl*, for example – arises not from a vulgar delight in their wealth, but from a profound understanding of the seductive and corrupting power of all the goods of this world.

What Eagleton dislikes, of course, is James's preoccupation with personal morality, his indifference to the workings of everyday life, and his complete lack of explicit ideological commitment. James followed Engels's precept: he wrote good novels, not socialist tracts. But this is no protection from a critical doctrine which is devoted to unearthing not what writers do but what they do not do. Dismissing *Portrait of a Lady* – that classic tale of possession and dispossession – as an insipid chronicle of 'civilized consciousness', Eagleton believes that there *is* an ideological commitment in James, but it is hidden or concealed, even from the author himself. His interest in morality is mere civilized consciousness is a sign of this commitment, for to the Marxist theoretician the notion of morality is like a red rag to a bull: one of the worst liberal humanist delusions which values the individual over the group and the personal over the political. James, in short, is part of the massive bourgeois conspiracy to conceal the real conditions of life (determined by economic relationships) in a fog of liberal humanist sentimentalizing about the romantic relationships of the rich, their trivial moral scruples, and so on, like a superior Barbara Cartland. The thing which distinguishes him from Miss Cartland – his technical virtuosity

– only confirms Eagleton's suspicions. Such virtuosity is a sort of conjuring trick distracting James and his readers from the really important business in hand, i.e., the class struggle.

As I have suggested, James has more, and more interesting, things to say about class than Eagleton himself, but the really interesting point here concerns Eagleton's 'explanation' of James in terms of what he does not do. Like de Manic deconstruction this form of Marxist ideological criticism not only gives the text priority over the author: it gives the critic priority over the text, by licensing him to determine what is missing from the text. In principle, this is not a new approach. Critics have always supplied information to make a text coherent: that is part of their function. To the extent that reading is interpretation, it involves adding to or subtracting from whatever is on the page. The difference is that de Man and Eagleton want to make their activities not suggestive – 'You might read it like this' – but prescriptive – 'That is what the text really means though the author didn't know it.' This is bafflingly paradoxical, because such prescriptive criticism is exactly what Eagleton claims to dislike in the bourgeois tradition. It also supports the view that, for all its recondite vocabulary, *Criticism and Ideology* is simply substituting a Marxist historical scheme for a traditional one.

The notion of the text's (or the critic's) 'hidden' ideology is most famously formulated in Macherey's *A Theory of Literary Production* where we find the doctrine of the 'non-dit' or 'silence'. Macherey believes that ideology is not merely a static configuration of beliefs characterizing any group but a dynamic process which reproduces itself (Althusser makes much the same point). In this sense, ideology works through readers to produce interpretations of texts, determining the limits of those interpretations. What the reader reads, there-fore, is not the text, but what ideology allows him to read. If I believe *Anna Karenina* to be a tragic story about adulterous love, that is because bourgeois ideology encourages me to believe in the significance of individuals and their relationships. A Marxist explanation – of the sort offered by Lenin – would show me that Tolstoy is 'really' about relations of subordination and domination in capitalist society – a fact unknown to Tolstoy himself, who thought he was a Christian.

What matters in this literary theory is what matters in psychoanalytic theory: the repressed. The critic acts like an analyst. He studies the symptoms of the text to see what they really mean. This approach has a lot to be said for it. As mentioned above, it is only an extension of traditional practices, without the limiting factor of common sense or abitrary notions of aesthetic unity. But Macherey is particularly scathing about critical methods which – like traditional psychoanalytic methods – depend on the assumption that the text, like the psyche, has a kind of hidden identity, uniformity and coherence which it is the critic's (or the analyst's) business to reveal. Such a view is typical of bourgeois society's need to conceal from itself its own inner contradictions. The Marxist critic will therefore reveal the contradictions, loose ends and paradoxes in the text, much as the Marxist theoretician shows them up in capitalist society, in which the 'repressed' is, of course, the proletariat. Macherey's work thus points to a triple alliance of literary criticism, psychoanalysis and politics which is very characteristic of theory in the 1960s, and which provides a foundation for a truly activist criticism. By revealing the contradictions in literary texts, the critic can play his part in undermining the monolithic structure of capitalist society and contribute directly to the revolution.

But this approach also has a lot to be said against it. To begin with, the belief that texts are altogether self-contradictory is as arbitrary as the assumption that they constitute coherent unities. Everything depends on the way in which they are read. Macherey's theory, whatever its claims, is not a scientific form of 'explanation' but another theory of reading, and interesting only as such. Furthermore, it doesn't tell me why I should read literature in the way he suggests:

that requires a prior decision about the meaning of history and an acceptance of Marxism's authority. But in order to arrive at that, I have already had to embark on interpretation – not of the text but of history. Only when I decide that – for example – what counts about the centuries since the end of feudalism is the class struggle, can I embark on a Machereyan analysis. For of course, Macherey does not want us to reinterpret our texts just anyhow. He doesn't want to substitute chaos for unity. What he does want to substitute, in my view, is another kind of concealed ideology, this time the ideology of Marxism, masquerading as superior truth. Literary interpretation is simply pushed back one stage, from the text to the context. Macherey and Eagleton are both keen on the distinction between interpretation (which is subjective and therefore bourgeois) and explanation (which is objective and therefore scientific) but this distinction is the merest fantasy. It assumes that history is a more objective study than criticism. This assumption stands on very weak grounds and it leads Marxist critics in a circle whereby they end up with the old-fashioned historical criticism or the old-fashioned genre criticism that the new Marxist theory was designed to replace.

The problem here is that there are only two limitations on interpretation. One is context. This can take many forms – convention and tradition, common-sense judgment, circumstances of interpretation etc. – but it is always relative: you can always make the text mean something else by changing the context. That is the basis of deconstruction. The other limitation is an appeal to objective truth. As a science of ideology which claims priority over other philosophical viewpoints, Marxism must establish this second kind of limitation. Without it, every Marxist 'explanation' can itself be interpreted ad infinitum. Marxists have the same problem as structuralists: they are trying to provide ultimate grounds for criticism, not just another critical perspective. Yet the very activity of establishing those grounds opens the way to reinterpretation. This is what we might call the theological problem – the problem of the Final Cause – and it seriously undermines Macherey's enterprise by making the Final Cause a Marxist interpretation of history – not because this interpretation is wrong, but because it is an interpretation and because it violates Macherey's own analytic principles by being a Hidden Force, an undeclared ultimate sanction.

Fredric Jameson has much the same problem in *The Political Unconscious*, a classic of recent RLT. Jameson is a dauntingly sophisticated writer who combines elements from Althusser, Lacan and Derrida in his attempt to construct a theory of narrative as symbolic action. Jameson is troubled about the status of the History (with a capital H) to which he refers. In particular he is disturbed by post-Saussurean claims, found at their most extreme in certain forms of deconstruction, that, just as we cannot 'know' the meaning of a text we cannot know the meaning of History: we can only rest briefly on this or that interpretation. This brings the Marxist notion of objective historical laws under severe strain. Even the weaker form of deconstruction implies that, while there may be such a thing as Truth, we have no sure access to it because the relation between language and anything it may express is so problematic. While accepting the importance of this problematic – it is, indeed, a plank of his theory – Jameson cannot go along with the view that History (or history) is just another text, another interpretation of interpretation, and he remarks, contemplating Althusser's critique of historical causality, that 'he does not at all draw the fashionable conclusion that because history is a text the "referent" does not exist. We would therefore propose the following revised formulation: that history is not a text . . . but that . . . it is inaccessible to us except in textual form.'[8]

One is tempted to ask Jameson if he seriously thinks that any rational person ever supposed anything else, but that would be to miss a larger point. For Jameson is not just talking about history in the sense of past events of which we can have knowledge only through records: he is also referring to History as the meaning or significance of the past, what it all adds up to. Indeed, for Jameson and other Marxists, there is no such thing as 'the past' in the neutral sense of 'what happened'. There is only History as meaning. This is why he has a problem with historical textuality: a text is something which signifies, events are just what happens. But it is because Jameson wants to conflate the two elsewhere – to claim that history is always History – that he is forced to separate them here. The problem for Marxists is that for History to mean something, there must be facts to be explained. But if all 'facts' are already interpretations there can be no objective explanation, and no appeal to History as the final ground of understanding.

Jameson tries to get round this by claiming that History (in the proper Marxist sense) is precisely what bourgeois society represses as the patient represses the cause of his symptoms. This is Macherey's 'non-dit'. History as Reality – as the meaning of Reality (i.e., the repression of the proletariat by the bourgeoisie, the class war etc.) – is what bourgeois culture conceals from us. The critic's task is to make this History explicit. The problems involved in such an operation become apparent as soon as Jameson departs from his lengthy theoretical exposition to embark on discussions of specific texts. Detailed commentaries on Balzac, Gissing and Conrad are brought in to support the theoretical argument. Jameson evidently admires *Nostromo* but thinks Conrad a fool – someone who, for all his great powers as a narrator, is less capable of saying what he means than Jameson himself. This is in line with the doctrine that the reader produces the text's meaning, but it runs up against the problem of History. For however elaborate Jameson's analysis, and however persuasive his demonstration that previous accounts of *Nostromo* have been corrupted by bourgeois ideology (and they are not very convincing), Jameson's skill goes for nothing unless we have already accepted a view of history and human life which goes clean counter not only to Conrad's own declared views but to seventy years of readerly opinion. The bizarre thing about this is that while Jameson lectures the reader on the importance of historical interpretation – ' "Always historicize" is the one transhistorical imperative of dialectical thought' – he blatantly ignores all the rules of historical analysis: paying attention to the text, for example, or having regard to the weight of evidence. Nor does Jameson extend his doubts about our ability to know history (except as a text) to texts themselves, which he confidently masters in his work. And although we cannot know history it seems that we can Know History, i.e., the meaning of events whose reality is itself uncertain.

Furthermore, Jameson – like Macherey and Eagleton – silently attributes to History the very qualities of unity, coherence, autonomy etc. he denies to literary texts and human identities, thus privileging it as a concept in a way highly suspect to the very RLT in whose name Jameson writes. He behaves, in other words, as though we all know what History is. This is a tactful way of avoiding the awkward fact that according to Jameson's own historicism and post-Saussurean linguistic theory, History is as much subject to contextual determination as any other concept – unless, of course, we refer it to old-fashioned humanistic notions of objectivity and reference. But that would be to 'recuperate' the concept, i.e., to think of it in a common-sense way unacceptable to RLT for whom common sense is another name for bourgeois mystification.

It seems that the only way out of this embarrassing circle is to invent a new language – what Jameson calls a mastercode. The language of radical theory is clearly a move towards such a code which would have a number of functions, including the creation of a common tongue for critical discourse – what Jameson rather awkwardly calls a mode in which 'structurally distinct objects (sic) or sectors of being' could be accommodated. Needless to say, any such language would be Marxist because only within Marxism are the horizons (limitations) of other codes transcended. And this in turn is possible because only Marxism has a complete explanation of History (the argument spirals round with dizzying speed) which, of course, includes all possible codes. Or as Jameson puts it, such a language would 'restore, at least methodologically, the lost unity of social life, and demonstrate that widely different elements of the social totality are ultimately part of the same global historical process'.[9]

And should the befuddled reader ask why it is either necessary or desirable that 'widely different elements within the social totality should be shown to be part of the same global process' (as though the postulation of a 'social totality' didn't already *assume* just that) – the answer is that this has to be the case if we are to make any sense of Marxist historiography. For the historical laws of Marxism (like Christian theology) only work within the context of a total view of History: a scheme of Fall and Redemption. Indeed, it is precisely Marxism's claim to pre-eminence – as it once was Christianity's – that it is the only ideology to give us a complete vision of History transcending all others (though how we can know this if we cannot stand outside Marxist ideology is a puzzle indeed).

We need to bear such claims in mind when approaching Jameson's theory. At first sight, it is a mystery why he should bother with literature at all in what is clearly a major cultural and political theory – let alone work out that theory through the detailed discussion of specific texts. His book is not 'about' Gissing, Conrad, or any of the other writers he discusses. They serve a larger purpose. The clue to their significance is to be found in Jameson's subtitle to *The Political Unconscious*, 'Narrative as a Socially Symbolic Act', which is also suggestive of the whole drift of RLT in recent years. Jameson derives his theory of symbolic acts from Kenneth Burke. As the phrase exactly suggests, a symbolic act is both an act, in that it tries to affect the world, and symbolic in the sense that it does so indirectly.

This formula, however, is only a starting-point, a problem not a solution. It brings us back to all the old questions about the relationship between textuality and reality, literature and interpretation, reference and signification. Jameson approaches these questions from the familiar RLT viewpoint. First, he takes it as axiomatic that literature's mimetic and expressive functions are marginal. He can do this because he believes, in common with many recent writers, that narrative is not imitative but constitutive. It has often been suggested that we make sense of the world by telling stories about it. Jameson wants to go further by suggesting that stories are a fundamental epistemological category, that reality is given to us in narrative form. This ties in very nicely with the Marxist way of looking at History, for if the world comes to us in stories, it follows that to change the stories we tell would be to change the world. It therefore allows us to intervene in History to change the story of our destiny.

This has important consequences for the critic as activist. If we can change History, there is no reason why we should not interfere with Literature. This process – often called rereading or rewriting – takes a number of forms. It can involve reinterpreting particular texts, giving a new account of literary history, reorganizing the canon of conventionally respected books and writers, altering academic syllabuses, changing the relationship between the academic study of literature and other disciplines, and so on. Jameson concentrates on the first, with surprising results. In the case of *Nostromo* and *Lord Jim*, he reads straight across the grain of the novelist's declared views and the narrator's. It is hard to see the justification for this. If textual evidence is to be ignored completely, the way is open for anyone to read anything in any way they like – and indeed some radical critics advocate just that. The pertinent objection (there are others) is that such a practice would effectively destroy literary studies as an academic discipline: without generally accepted methodological rules, however loosely applied, it could not survive. I am not so sure that this would be a bad thing – but I am very sure that the critics who advocate a hermeneutic free-for-all would be indignant if redundancy were the outcome.

Jameson's rewriting of Conrad is not gratuitous: it is meant as a serious example of what reinterpretation involves when the hidden ideology – what Jameson calls the repressed History – of the text is revealed. Jameson wants to show us that when Conrad writes nostalgically about conservatism or old-fashioned standards of honour and courtesy which, as the Marxist knows, could only exist because the honourable and courteous were funded by a toiling proletariat, he is suffering from a form of bad faith, false consciousness or ideological delusion which we can show if we analyse the text from our superior ideological vantage-point. This is not necessarily arrogance on Jameson's part: he allows that those who come after us will be in a position to analyse our bad faith from their superior vantage-point, as will their successors ad infinitum. There is no way out of ideology, only steps on the way upwards (though how we can know it is the way upwards is another puzzle). But his approach does involve him in a hopeless contradiction. We can see this if we ask ourselves why he concentrates on Conrad as the novelist of late nineteenth-century imperial adventure rather than, say, Haggard or Henty. The answer is that Jameson just thinks Conrad is a better novelist. But on what basis does he think Conrad is a better novelist if his novels need rewriting before they are acceptable? If the critic blatantly ignores what the text actually says in favour of what he wants it to say?

The contradiction here is that on the one hand, Jameson is prepared to accept Conrad at that novelist's bourgeois valuation as one of the great writers of the bourgeois tradition – to which Jameson is entirely committed – while on the other he wants to say simultaneously (1) that Conrad rises above that tradition in ways Haggard doesn't, and (2) that the values which support that tradition (the values of liberal humanism) are meaningless. In other words, he wants to detach Conrad from the very context which makes him significant both as a 'great novelist' and as a suitable subject for academic study, while relying on that context to give force to his analysis.

Other radical theorists, pondering this contradiction, have concluded that reinterpreting literary classics is not enough. On the contrary, it is dangerously prone to lead away from revolutionary activity and straight back into bourgeois practices of interpretation. Something more thorough-going is needed – a complete reassessment not of individual texts but of literature's history and status. Eagleton and others believe that the very idea of 'literature' as a privileged domain is the immediate cause of the trouble, and a characteristic sign of capitalism's drive to alienation through the separation and isolation of different discourses. For them a theory of literature as symbolic action only makes sense if it is more closely allied with direct institutional action. This can range from changing academic syllabuses to a wholesale reorganization of literary education as a part of (and contributing to) the transformation of society.

In the absence of full political involvement, however, the symbolic act theory justifies critics in operating at the level of literary studies themselves: changing these can be their contribution to the revolution until the opportunity comes for fuller participation. If changing stories is changing the world, the key to this activity is changing the story of literary studies. In Chapter 2 we saw one example of how Eagleton approaches this task in his account of the relationship between the history of criticism and the history of capitalist society. Another approach involves rewriting the canon. This is a particular favourite among English and American radicals still reeling under the influence of Leavis's obsession with literary value-judgments. Leavis is the stern father to whom most anglophone critics are still in an Oedipal relation, endlessly struggling to get away from his influence only to find themselves repeating his example. The attempts of Eagleton and Belsey to rewrite the canon are typical. In *Criticism and Ideology* Eagleton simply turns father's doctrines on their heads. Leavis's heroes become Eagleton's villains. Radical variants of the Brontës (conspicuously omitted from *The Great Tradition*) are substituted for George Eliot, James, Conrad and Lawrence, and the canonical train rolls on. Belsey, under the influence of feminism, is more thoroughgoing in her radicalism. She proposes to dispense with the canon entirely, or at least to vary it with the introduction of writers hitherto considered minor. But in practice she, too, falls prey to the curse of the Doctor's Tomb: Conan Doyle is cited only to be crushed, and Dr Belsey gets back to the proper academic business of writing books about Milton.

There is a real problem here – namely that the very existence of the literary academy which validates their activities is closely bound up with traditions, however extensively rewritten. To take the drastic step of burning Raphael (and every literary equivalent), as Mayakovsky suggested in the immediate aftermath of the Russian Revolution, would be to destroy the critical institution, and that would mean the end of any effective base for RLT. The alternative is to do something about the existing machinery – to rebuild the boat at sea, in Quine's often quoted phrase – by transforming the academy itself into what radicals sometimes call 'a site of struggle': an opportunity to wage war on the bourgeoisie in its own territory. Theory, too, is such a site, revaluation of tradition one weapon in the war.

Marxism is traditionally much concerned with the problem of value, and the domain of literary value seems a suitable area for it to attack. As we have seen in the case of Jameson, many theorists sidestep the issue by accepting bourgeois valuations of texts for which they provide new explanations, and Marxist sociologies of literature have proved woefully inadequate to answer that troubling question: why do we value one text more than another? In general terms, the answer has to do with ideological predisposition – we value a text because it embodies the prejudices of the ruling class, or – more subtly – because it expresses the dominant ideology; but such formulations are circular and useless, productive of that critical poverty which is reduced to pigeon-holing texts according to their ideological content. As we can see in Jameson or Eagleton, the sophistication with which this content is analysed bears no relation whatever to the ultimate critical judgment of the text under discussion: it remains obstinately an account of ideology, not of literature. Nor does it give us adequate reasons for preferring one text to another within the same ideological scheme – for preferring, say, *Portrait of a Lady* to *Watch and Ward*.

One way round this problem is to dismiss it as irrelevant. According to this argument, the hierarchy of traditional critical values – whether expressed in the choice of preferred classic texts or in the selection of important features in those texts – simply repeats and supports the bourgeois social hierarchy which produced it in the first place. This hierarchy is organized in favour of the ruling class and against oppressed 'minorities' which include women, children, blacks, homosexuals and virtually everyone who is not a white, heterosexual, Caucasian, bourgeois male or his hanger-on. The ruling class prescribes what literature shall be valued, how it shall be taught and what interpretation shall be put upon it (this is done through the teaching), and it naturally prefers those texts, or aspects of texts, which show it and its values up in a favourable light. The large numbers of women and homosexuals (and latterly blacks) who have contributed to this literary tradition can be shown either to have unconsciously absorbed the dominant ideology and/or to have suffered at its hands. The evidence for this is available in two forms: (1) a deconstruction of the contradictions and stresses in specific appropriate texts; and (2) by appeal to the great mass of forgotten or 'hidden' comparable texts 'suppressed' by the dominant ideology. Emily Brontë is a favourite example here. Most recent accounts of *Wuthering Heights* go to great lengths to relate the oppression of nineteenth-century English women to the complexities and ambiguities of the novel's narrative structure and ideological formations. This is not done in the vulgar biographical sense, of course, but by appeal to the ideological contradictions in which Emily was involved by virtue of being a woman in a chauvinist society. This is clear in a wide range of non-canonical texts by contemporary women who shared Emily's predicament. *Wuthering Heights* makes more sense in relation to them than it does in the context of a chronological sequence – which is precisely why it had to be excluded by Leavis.

One might well argue that this is not so much a deconstruc-tion of the canon as an expansion of it – and the massive reprinting of once-forgotten novels in recent years supports such a view. Nineteenth-century female writers do not stay in print merely because of antiquarian or scholarly interest: they have to earn their keep. It will be interesting to see how many recent discoveries hold the market. They have yet to dislodge classic texts from the canon of academically approved works except in a few isolated cases, or where the study of literature has given way to media or discourse studies of which literary texts form only one·part. This is the solution to the problems of the literary academy advocated by many Marxists, who want to see the humane disciplines replaced by the study of ideology in all its cultural forms. It is hard to see how this differs from conventional criticism except in the disturbing narrowness of its focus and the absurd naïvety of its precon-ception that culture is simply a delusion to be exposed – a preconception symmetrical with its equally absurd prede-cessor: that art is the privileged receptacle of truth.

But one can also argue that such a deconstruction or expansion of the canon is really an evasion of the vital theoretical issue here. By dismissing evaluation as a bourgeois irrelevance and insisting that what matters about a text – or a tradition – is not its value but what we make of it (i.e., that its value is determined by its function and not vice versa) RLT does not dispose of the problem: it merely relocates it from the text to its context. We are then faced with the problem of describing and evaluating contexts, and criticism turns into the sociology of literature, which within radical Marxism is another name for the study of ideology. The paradox – as always with RLT – is that we stop studying literature in order to do something else. 'Literature' as a category disappears – or, as Eagleton suggests, never existed in the first place.

This is a typical example of the RLT Midas syndrome. Just as everything structuralists touch turns into structures and everything deconstructors touch turns into rhetoric, so everything Marxists touch turns into ideology. And we know what happened to Midas. When everything is gold, gold loses its value and becomes a curse. The purpose of 'Literature' as a concept, however loosely defined, is to make useful working distinctions, not to set up insuperable barriers between literature and non-literature. By following his usual practice of simply turning conventional terms on their head, Eagleton remains trapped by them. 'What is literature?' has never been a very interesting or significant question at the best of times. Now it matters only to radical theorists determined to show that Literature is an example of Capitalism's drive to set up ruling ideas. It is one of the instruments used by the bourgeoisie to assert their ascendancy by excluding the proletariat from Culture, or demanding that they acquire Culture only on bourgeois terms. No doubt there is something in this view when considered in the context of nineteenth- and twentieth-century European schools and colleges which enforced a hierarchical view of Serious and Popular Art (which rarely corresponded with the distinction between good and bad art). No doubt Eagleton experienced his own form of this hierarchy at the hands of Leavisite schoolteachers, who associated

Art with moral improvement and elitist social and political attitudes. But to limit the idea of literature to such a context is absurd. Since antiquity there have been debates about the quality and value of different sorts of writing, and the distinction between trivia and High Art: Aristophanes for one has a good deal to say on the subject. And it is from these debates that literary criticism derives its existence. Simply announcing that literature (with or without a capital L) no longer exists, will not put a stop to them. On the contrary, when they cease, criticism will no longer be of interest as an academic study and there will be no need to say anything at all.

What Eagleton's announcement does do is to underline the radical view that a change in language is also a change in reality: abolishing the concept of literature is the same as abolishing the thing itself. This is made possible by the doctrine that reality is constituted in rhetorical forms – stories, models and metaphors – and that the principal medium of these forms is language. Change your metaphor, according to this argument, and you change your world. And this is the key to linking interpretation and action, criticism and revolution. The critic becomes an epistemological advance guard, urging his audience to alter not just their view of what literature represents but the very form and meaning of that representation. Thus even if bourgeois ideology gives an accurate account of reality as it is, we can change that reality. But where peasants once tried to do it by storming the Winter Palace, intellectuals can now achieve the same end more effectively from the comfort of their armchairs.

Yet in the end, short of imposing the critical equivalent of Stalinist terror to impose their ideas, it is hard to see how Marxist critics can make this prescription work, for they are still bound by the constraints which bind every critic, who must persuade his readers that his account of a text conforms to its reality in some shape or form (and these may be very varied). And this very conformity presupposes a distance

141

between reality and interpretation which is precisely what radical Marxists are trying to get away from in their theories of ideology. The problem with Jameson's work, for example, is that he wants at the same time to say that our reality is constituted by narratives, and that his interpretation of those narratives conforms with certain objectively true historical laws which stand above or apart from them.

Ironically, then, the radical Marxist project can only succeed insofar as it accepts what Marxists themselves define as bourgeois notions of objectivity, interpretation and criticism. Its 'scientific' explanations are merely forms of interpretation, its political activism a new form of traditional critical pretensions to cultural and social authority. For a truly radical, i.e., subversive, criticism, it seems we must look elsewhere.

6

Girls on Top

> Another of de Selby's weaknesses was his
> inability to distinguish between men and
> women . . .

I have saved feminism for the end of this discussion not to
please or annoy feminists – who may find in its belatedness
either the consoling last word or chauvinist relegation – but
to suit myself. It is in feminist theory that the difficulties of
evolving a convincingly politicized critical pedagogy are most
dramatically focused. Not that all feminist theorists are full-
blooded radicals, of course: they cover the spectrum from
political revolutionaries, out to destroy the bourgeois order,
to social reformers who see human progress as a matter of
getting more women into good academic jobs. But most of
them share the view that the literary academy is primarily a
political arena, and that the view of it I have been espousing
– as a place where learning how to think involves cultivating
detachment, neutrality and objectivity in the investigation of
all and any ideas – is not only characteristically bourgeois
but typically male. It is an adjunct to what feminists like to
call patriarchal ideology, or patriarchy: a complex of ideas
founded on the equation between masculinity, rationality,
and the social, cultural and political institutions of the
Western democracies. The objective of feminist theory is to
prise open this ideology as it is manifested in literature and
literary studies. This is another form of the ideological
critique discussed in the last three chapters, and in many
ways it is the most powerful and far-reaching. The conceptual
analysis of structuralism and deconstruction is remote from

the interests of most readers, and even the visceral appeal of Marxism can be muted by the complex theoretical apparatus in which it is often involved these days. But the most misogynistic of men (and women) encounter the basic material of feminist theory – male–female relations, masculine–feminine contrasts – in their own lives. They experience them at first hand.

Among liberal feminists it is often this very experience which provides a theoretical foundation. Elaine Showalter, for example, has written about the problems of establishing a feminist theory in terms of the conflicts between socio-sexual characteristics.[1] She sees her project as a matter of reconciling private and public, personal and political, empirical and theoretical, given a traditional context in which the first term in each pair is thought of as characteristically feminine, the second as masculine. On the one hand, it is the business of feminist theory to question these oppositions. On the other, testimony confirms that women are more often made feminists by experience than by logical (i.e., 'masculine') argument. Not unnaturally, they tend to make this experience the basis of their cultural and political theory, and even to believe that defining a certain type of experience is the best way of defining female being in the world.

The problem with this argument is its circularity. It depends upon the assumption that there is such a thing as 'female experience' and that it differs in specific ways from male experience. Some feminists, observing this difficulty (Showalter is not one of them), go further, claiming that experience as such is typically female, males (for whatever reason) tending to abstraction and conceptualization (such activities not being deemed experiences). This unlikely distinction, common among French radical feminists, is playfully symbolized in the form of the Greek letter 'phi' which suggests the link between philosophy – the characteristic mode of abstraction – and the phallus.

At this point, all sorts of logical complications arise, many

144

of them deriving from uncertainties about the relationship between biological gender (male/female) and sexuality (feminine/masculine) and the extent to which the first distinction does or does not determine the second. More to the point, there is a particular difficulty for feminists who want to construct a literary theory, for insofar as theory apes or resembles philosophy, it can be seen as 'phallocentric' (i.e., male/masculine), excluding or marginalizing women, even when they are its subject. Feminist theoreticians thus find themselves involved in a paradox if they want to claim for female experience an authenticity and authority beyond the imperial reach of theory. In other words: how is female experience (however we define it) to be theorized without denying its very nature?

Liberal feminists such as Showalter take their stand on the Leavisite belief that literature is by nature the home of experience as opposed to theory. This is simply an empirical fact. They claim that in books by and about women – many of them ignored, forgotten or even suppressed – we can find a record of women's experience which the literary academy – as an arm of patriarchy – has consistently devalued. The task of feminist critics is to rediscover such books and to rewrite literary history to take account of them. Theory's job is to provide them with an armoury of concepts to justify this practice.

Showalter herself has done just that in *A Literature of Their Own* which has subsequently had many imitators. The point of her book is to reassess the women writers who have always been considered major in the context of many rediscoveries, and to identify different phases of women's writing as aspects of their social and political evolution. *A Literature of Their Own* thus challenges patriarchy on what are seen to be its own grounds: the manipulation of literary history in the particular form of the canon of texts approved for academic study. For Showalter is not just concerned to reclaim forgotten masterpieces: one purpose of her rewriting is to prompt a reorganization of the literary syllabus in the name of social justice. What this involves is explained in a prize-winning essay by Annette Kolodny, reprinted in one of Showalter's own collections.[2] Kolodny believes that feminist criticism 'finally coheres in its stance of almost defensive re-reading',[3] i.e., that its task is to reinterpret the past in the service of contemporary political requirements, and she sets out to force her 'adversaries' (chauvinist male critics) either to accept her reinterpretation or at least to accept the partiality of their own judgments. She does this in terms of three propositions, which are meant to serve as axioms for the new critical theory.

These axioms are well worth considering, uniting as they do the three topics of RLT which have been the focus of this book: interpretation, textuality and ideology. They also depend on the assumptions – fundamental to RLT – that criticism is necessarily political, and that 'political' means self-interested. The argument here seems to be that politics is about conflicts between sexes and classes, and that it is a liberal deception to suppose that such conflicts have been or ever can be successfully resolved in the context of bourgeois society. The only honest criticism (and theory) therefore displays its prejudices and sharpens the conflicts either to precipitate their ultimate resolution in a socialist state or (and this is Kolodny's view, which turns out to be a new form of classical liberalism with the grounding concepts removed) to remind us that there are no objective or consensual values, only differences.

Her three propositions are:

(1) literary history (and with that the historicity of literature) is a fiction;

(2) insofar as we are taught how to read, what we engage are not texts but paradigms;

(3) since the grounds upon which we assign aesthetic value to texts are never infallible, unchangeable or universal, we must re-examine not only our aesthetics

146

but, as well, the inherent biases and assumptions informing the critical methods which (in part) shape our aesthetic responses.[4]

It is unfortunate but typical that in constituting the ground for a feminist aesthetic these propositions deny the very thing which makes that aesthetic necessary, i.e., the real and absolute (not fictional or relative) injustice done to literature by and about women. Let us take them in order.

(1) The assertion that literary history (or any other kind of history) is a fiction is now a familiar radical commonplace, but the meaning becomes no clearer with repetition. Presumably Kolodny is not denying the historical existence of the past. She thinks Shakespeare existed, that some plays were written before others, that they contain more or less interesting verifiable references to contemporary circumstances. There is, of course, scope for argument about the function, status and accuracy of such facts, and wide latitude for scholarly speculation which can sometimes be satisfied by external or internal evidence and sometimes not. So much is commonplace. The question is whether we accept the authenticity of such information. There seems little point in denying it: a complete scepticism renders the whole critical and scholarly enterprise futile (which it may be). It also puts Kolodny out of her chair and undermines the feminist project itself. If literary history is a fiction, why is feminism not a fiction?

Kolodny has a problem here with the word 'fiction', when the word she wants is, of course, interpretation. What worries her is the equation of literary history with the official academic canon, the body of texts deemed worthy of study at any one moment. This equation she attributes to her opponents, who use it to exclude from history what they regard as non-canonical, including texts by women. Her point is that there are alternative histories and therefore alternative canons.

Even if we accept this point it is hard to see why these alternatives should be called fictions – a move which makes them all – the feminist canon included – equally arbitrary. But I do not know that I am inclined to accept it. When the closed corpus of Greek and Latin literature formed the basis of literary study it was perhaps possible to identify history and the canon, though even within this closed corpus discriminations were made: Virgil ranked higher than the poets of the Greek Anthology. Yet has there ever been a time when one single canon was generally accepted? Is the feminist struggle to open it up really so heroically new? Even the Greeks argued fiercely about the relative merits of their writers – we have the testimony in Aristophanes – and recent attempts to impose a canon (Arnold, Leavis, Eliot) have all been highly controversial. The canon is a regulative not a constitutive principle of literary studies. As such, it has been subject to constant revision. This has been slower in some ages than in others. In our own time the changes seem to occur from hour to hour. This may be a good thing.

One can argue, I suppose, about whether a regulative principle is the same as an enabling fiction – but the use of the word fiction in this context strikes me as gratuitously confusing. Presumably Kolodny thinks there is a body of *real* women's writing which is *really* hidden from view and that there are *real* reasons for its concealment and for the importance of reviving it – reasons she connects with the *real* predicament of *real* women in the *real* world – otherwise she wouldn't be so excited about this issue. These texts are part of literary history. Some ways of interpreting that history foreground them, others do not – but an interpretation is not the same as a fiction. The first is constrained by context – by real circumstances; the second isn't.

The problem of what constitutes history arises for Kolodny because of the familiar radical confusion about how we understand it. Talking about canons and fictive histories, for example, she tells us at one moment that these are of 'our own making' and then, in the very next breath, that they are produced by the 'critical ideology' which is outside our control. Needless to say, canons (and historical interpretations) are neither freely chosen nor completely determined: they grow out of the interplay between the material available and the use we make of it. What makes them significant is their occupation of the puzzling ground where we try to make disinterested sense out of brute circumstance, such as historical facts.

This is partly the point Kolodny is denying, of course, in her claim that the historicity of literature is also a fiction. Her argument is not easy to disentangle. She seems to be making several points at once, including the old chestnut that we cannot know an author's intentions. But this is subordinate to the more general assertion that all we do when we read is recognize literary conventions. On the one hand, literature gives us no information about the past; on the other hand, there is no point in studying it in historical context because this context – like the relationships between texts – is simply another fiction we make up at will or passively accept from the ruling ideology.

If true, this renders all scholarship in the human sciences futile. When the only reason for studying the history of a subject is to justify our own prejudices in the present, the money is wasted. But, of course, it is not true. Why should Kolodny think we can know the present when we cannot know the past, or recognize 'literary conventions' when we cannot recognize anything else in the text? It is a strange cognitive distinction which denies us the knowledge of our own experience (unless we are women) but allows us the knowledge of highly specialized literary artifices. I can't understand Oedipus's feelings about incest – but I can scrape acquaintance with the significance of the parados in Greek tragedy. Very strange.

Even stranger that literature apparently cannot do what every other cultural phenomenon can do, i.e., throw some light on the past when considered in context. Works of art are a source of evidence no more and no less valuable than other artefacts. Like cups and saucers they are made for use, and we can deduce something tentative from this usage. Here again the distinction between interpretation and fiction must be applied. What Shakespeare's chronicle plays tell us about attitudes to power and authority in late sixteenth-century England can be confirmed from other sources. Such evidence is in no way final – but if Kolodny's female authors are allowed to express their concerns in their texts, why exclude everyone else? Kolodny is quite content to draw simple conclusions about the women's writing she discusses while imposing the most ridiculously sophisticated criteria on others. In the matter of making historical fictions, she certainly practises what she preaches, blithely relegating the past which has made all of us what we are to the realm of convenient myths, thereby devaluing the very literature she wants to exalt. For if literature's past is simply a matter of our choice, why should we bother with books (e.g., nineteenth-century American women novelists) which are not to our taste? If this is a moral duty – and Kolodny thinks it is – then its authority must be grounded precisely in a distinction between mere taste or self-interest and some higher objective obligations, i.e., to respect equal rights; and these obligations must in turn be founded upon a belief in the real history of injustice to women and women's literature.

(2) The confusion between fiction and interpretation leads Kolodny – as she confesses with shy pride – to her next proposition: that because we can only read paradigms we 'appropriate meaning from a text according to what we need (or desire)'.[5] Quite why we should do this in literature when we learn from painful experience not to do it in life, Kolodny does not make clear. Her proposal would seem to imply that our experience of texts is essentially trivial: it doesn't matter what we make of them, because our literary views have no

consequences. What I appropriate from *War and Peace*, say, has no bearing on other aspects of my life. But such a conclusion would contradict Kolodny's belief that literature is a social institution, and that we read in it, if not the world's reflection, at least the image of our ways of looking at it. The contradiction is enough to render her second proposition incoherent, even if experience did not tell us that we subordinate our interpretations to common goals as much as our political aspirations – which is not to say that we don't appropriate meaning from a text, only that such appropriations take place within narrowly defined limits, and that differences are usually minor matters of emphasis.

More to the point, the concept of such appropriation is not a coherent starting-place for academic literary study. It simply has the effect of extending one stage further the Marxist move to transfer attention from the text to the cultural and political context. Kolodny's approach would invite us, like a form of psychoanalysis, to attend to readerly desire. If Marxism turns criticism into ersatz sociology, this kind of feminism turns it into ersatz therapy, whose logical terminus is the unbounded subjectivity of psychosis: an inability to distinguish between ourselves and the world, between fact and fiction, truth and lies, literature and reality. This is precisely the object of RLT in its zanier manifestations. But if all literary facts (irrespective of their status) are fictions, what is the use of the fact/fiction distinction? And why bother to distinguish between Lukács's view of Balzac, and that of the madman who thinks he *is* Balzac?

Kolodny's emphasis on reading as mastery of the paradigms is one way of maintaining this distinction. While the madman – rather like the bourgeois critic in radical mythology – thinks that there is only one meaning in a text and that he has the secret of it, the superior critic knows that every reading is just one more application of the paradigms. What is more, the value of these paradigms is determined entirely by their function. When the feminist reads a text, she is motivated not by the need to find out what it does or what it is about, but by a higher non-literary principle: improving the political situation of women. In common with many feminists, Kolodny thinks that because interpretation is *affected* by desire, it should be *determined* by it: because my understanding of *Paradise Lost* is shaped in part by my personal and social circumstances, these must be given hermeneutic priority.

The unstated argument here – which is characteristic of RLT in its politicized forms – seems to go something like this. Women's rights, or class rights, or whatever political nostrum it may be, are more important in the end than the study of literature. *Therefore* they should determine the academic study of that literature. The error lies not in the first proposition, but in the link between the two. To be fair to Kolodny, she is not insisting on a politicized academy in the sense that she wants teaching to be ideologically determined in her favour. On the contrary, she seems to be advocating a kind of Barthesian free play in which literary education will amount to the acquisition of as many paradigms as possible. Like Barbara Johnson, she thinks that teaching literature is teaching reading, and her notion of paradigms is not unlike Johnson's account of rhetoric. But by insisting on the intrinsically political nature of literary discourse on the one hand, and preaching pedagogic pluralism on the other, Kolodny loses out on both counts. The pluralism contradicts the politics. To concede it is to concede that feminism is just another paradigm, another way of reading texts, on a level with myth criticism or structuralism. It is, in other words, to forgo the very moral authority which gives feminist criticism its ideological claim to consideration.

Kolodny's problem here is that while her libertarian outlook makes her favour the idea of multiple viewpoints, she has no conception of these viewpoints meaning anything real to anyone except those who already hold them. She has, in short, no concept of imagination as sympathetic identification

152

or as genuinely entering into the life of others. She seems to assume that for every reader all viewpoints other than his own will have the same status as interpretive paradigms: alien machines which one learns to manipulate with more or less skill – much as Kolodny herself, according to her own account, painfully learnt to 'read' *Paradise Lost* by mastering epic conventions and the niceties of Christian theology. This sits with her claim that 'we read well and with pleasure what we already know how to read'.[6] Leaving aside what reading 'well' means in this context – mastery of the paradigms? – we can only wonder what 'already' signifies. In one way it appears to mean 'after we are thoroughly versed in the appropriate paradigms'. This implies that the best readers – those who read well – are products of Graduate School. But there also seems to be a hint that we can only truly 'read' what we *are* – that a text about women will only reveal its deepest significance to other women, a text about Marxism to other Marxists, and so on. This is indeed one justification for envisaging criticism as an arena of conflicting interests in which mutually incomprehensible opponents slug it out, but if so, it presents fearsome pedagogic problems. Teaching, like reading, conventionally presupposes communication. But what is to happen if male professors can never really grasp what feminist critics are saying (and vice versa) because no one can gain access to an understanding they do not already have, except in the debased form of a paradigm? What is the point of different parties even trying to make sense of one another in such a case? And how did they acquire the understanding they do have in the first place?

Kolodny lets herself off this hook with the ambiguous phrase, 'insofar as we learn how to read', but this just opens vistas on to huge problems in the field of cognitive science. Kolodny may be equipped to cope with these: most critics are not. And while it may be the case that in such a science we would find the true explanation for the male neglect of Charlotte Gilman Perkins – misunderstanding rather than poor literary quality (assuming these to be mutually exclusive) – the theory turns against Kolodny herself when, by the same lights, she explains her inability, as a Jewish feminist, to appreciate Milton properly. Such arguments, meant to promote pluralism, lead with equal ease to a self-defeating solipsism, as each reader, locked in her own uncertainly apprehended experience, fails to see the point of every other reader. Quite how such readers can even know when they do encounter a sympathetic text is another of Kolodny's mysteries. What such solipsism leaves us with is an unbridgeable gap beween the experience literature embodies and which limits its accessibility, and the teachable paradigms which allow us to read at all. This gap has to be closed by invoking a critical relativism which is, by the terms of Kolodny's own theory, futile. There can only be a sense of what is relative where there is a high degree of mutual understanding – precisely what Kolodny denies.

(3) This point is taken up in her third proposition, which seems at first sight to be the most acceptable – and the most traditional. What could be more commonplace and less controversial than the requirement that the critic subject her own premises to scrutiny? If there is one point on which radical theories, however avowedly scientific, agree, it is the view that all these premises are inherently and inevitably biased. The scrutiny Kolodny wants is therefore not a quest for greater truth or objectivity: it is not a matter of correcting biases so that one reduces them. Instead, we simply want to know what they are, so that we can substitute one for another, according to caprice or desire. The grounds of aesthetic value, after all, are 'never infallible, unchangeable or universal' – except, of course, for the claim that they are not. That alone is an infallible, unchangeable and universal principle of radical theory.

There are many problems with proposition (3), not least its extreme vagueness. If all values are relative, it is hard to see by what means – and for what purpose – one might evaluate the bias of aesthetic judgment. If the only criterion is to be need or desire (as established by proposition (2)), there is presumably no need to adjust our judgment relative to external standards (i.e., the biases of others); only insofar as it deviates from that need or desire – always assuming we can know what that need or desire is other than by way of the very judgments which embody it. And it is hard to see how we can know what *those* are except by reference to a publicly validated discourse, which would provide us with an external standpoint for judgment. Yet it is precisely the possibility of such a discourse Kolodny denies under propositions (1) and (2). There is no common critical language, no common experience, no historical point of reference, not even an Arnoldian touchstone to refer to. Only 'literary conventions which have survived through time' are left to the critic as his or her legitimate material for study. The rest belongs to semiology, psychology, cognitive science, sociology, anthropology etc.

Nor can these conventions in themselves provide any grounds for all but the most limited aesthetic judgment. Indeed, given Kolodny's dismissal of the historical context, it is difficult to imagine by what means one might estimate the relative success or failure of their deployment. This might be possible with a technical form such as the sonnet, governed by complex explicit rules and providing us with thousands of examples. On the other hand, one could easily produce a technically perfect sonnet of no other merit. And in the case of larger, less clearly defined forms, such as tragedy, the problems of relating technical conventions to intrinsic interest are notorious. Aristotle's *Poetics* – to take only one famous example – are worse than useless without an historical sense of what tragedy meant for the Greeks – a sense derived partly from Aristotle himself, partly from testimony, and partly from the small body of tragic texts we still possess. The admitted uncertainty and provisionality of such understanding as we have, does not contradict this point: it merely reminds us of the cognitive status of aesthetic understanding, which is neither fictional (as Kolodny seems to claim) nor factual (in the view she implicitly attributes to her opponents) but on a perplexing other ground whose very elusiveness is what makes it important. In short, understanding of conventions in itself, however detailed, is of no help without historical context.

The curious thing is that Kolodny's own essay admits as much when, towards the end, it appears that her 'fictionalism' isn't what it seemed to be, and the critic comes clean about her own real, external, historical standard of aesthetic judgment. That standard – which is, of course, the *raison d'être* for this essay in particular and feminist criticism in general – is the point at which 'female self-consciousness turns in upon itself, attempting to grasp the deepest conditions of its own unique and multiplicitous realities'.[7] So it seems that the reality earlier denied to the history and historicity of literature is to be granted to female self-consciousness in its literary moments of self-knowledge. History is a fiction: self-consciousness is the only reality.

But even more curious is the mildness of the critical prescription which follows on this triumph of solipsism, in marked contrast to the essay's initial boldness, and the passage is worth quoting in full, so typical is it of what radical theory boils down to when the rhetoric is stripped away.

> All the feminist is asserting . . . is her right to choose which features of the text she takes as relevant, because she is, after all, asking new and different questions of it. In the process she claims neither definitiveness nor stuctural completeness for her different readings and reading systems, but only their usefulness in recognizing the particular achievements of

woman as author, and their applicability in conscientiously decoding woman-as-sign.[8]

I like that 'conscientiously' – so serious, so American, so unnecessary. And who could object to this modest prescription? We may have doubts about the curious circularity of this critical method – the way in which Kolodny proposes to select only those 'features of the text' which give the right answers to the questions she wants to ask – answers which have been determined in advance of the questions. We may also wonder why such modest aims have to be asserted – given the critical free-for-all in progress over the last thirty years. And we may be perplexed about the possible criteria for choosing appropriate textual features, given Kolodny's earlier insistence that only 'literary conventions' remain recognizable through time. Surely it isn't features of the text she will choose first, but features of feminist theory which can then be applied to the text?

But these quibbles pale into insignificance beside the contradiction Kolodny is – ironically – involved in by her very modesty. At the beginning of this chapter I suggested that liberal-radical feminists had a problem reconciling the priority of experience with the law of theory – and this problem underpins the whole of 'Dancing Through the Minefield', which ends not with a bang but a whimper. For the contrast between the stern radical scepticism of her beginning and the critical quietism of her close suggests that Kolodny wants to have it both ways. She wants academic respectability (as a professor at Renssalaer Polytechnic Institute) and freedom from academic constraints. She wants a theoretical discourse for feminism which doesn't involve any theory. She wants to be radical without being political. She wants to make truth claims about the situation of women without accepting the validity of truth claims in general. She wants to write a history of women's writing while denying the reality of history. The list of contradictions might be extended, but as it happens, Kolodny herself sums them up for us in a poem by Adrienne Rich approvingly quoted at the end of her essay – a poem in which

> Vision begins to happen in such a life
> as if a woman quietly walked away
> from the argument and jargon in a room
> and sitting down in the kitchen began
>   turning in her lap
> bits of yarn, calico and velvet scraps,
>
> pulling the tenets of a life together
> with no mere will to mastery
> only care for the many-lived, unending
> forms in which she finds herself.[9]

Thus Kolodny allows herself to walk away from the argument and jargon at the moment of her own choosing – a well-tested means of having the last theoretical word. But the argument is not so much abandoned as postponed. The 'I'm not going to play this silly male game any more' move is only acceptable when it isn't followed by the player rejoining the game on her own terms, which is what Kolodny wants to do. Unfortunately we cannot make our own terms: the critical debate is a simulacrum of the real world in which we are constrained by real circumstances beyond our control. In the critical debate these 'circumstances' take the form of institutions, traditions and other people's opinions, all of which have to be taken into account if we want to play. The alternative is simply to talk to oneself, which is one serious possibility in feminist theory.

As Toril Moi points out, this is all very well but it goes against the whole point of a political criticism, which is to persuade others to one's point of view.[10] Moi criticizes Kolodny's relativism on the grounds that it provides no standpoint for distinguishing qualitatively between one theory and another, and brands her critical pluralism a liberal cop-out, a new form of aestheticism which evades the central theoretical issue which for Marxist feminists like Moi is the unmasking of ideology. Kolodny's exhortation to self-appraisal in proposition (3) is a very poor substitute for rigorous analysis, and in the end her theory, according to Moi, adds up to little more than a variation on the old bourgeois theme of interpretation. What feminist critics need is not merely an empirical method of ideological symptomatology (such as the 'Images of Women' criticism popular in America) but a general theory of cultural values.

The belief that there are no value-free judgments is a commonplace of radical theory. Kolodny herself remarks that 'If feminist criticism calls anything into question it must be that dog-eared myth of intellectual neutrality',[11] while Moi asserts that the radical critic's task is to 'make explicit the politics of the so-called neutral or objective work of their colleagues',[12] by whom she means, needless to say, liberal males. Judith Fetterly announces even more positively that 'feminist criticism is a political act whose aim is not simply to interpret the world but to change it by changing the consciousness of those who read and their relationship to what they read'.[13]

As we saw in the previous chapter, the turn from interpretation to action is not the straightforward business Fetterly's allusion to Marx would imply, especially if there is no possibility of objective standards by which to measure the changes action is supposed to produce. My account of Kolodny suggested that for the most part, feminists do have such standards based on a simple political morality of right and wrong barely concealed behind their sophisticated cultural relativism. Liberation is right, oppression is wrong, radicalism is right, tradition wrong, equality is right, hierarchy wrong, and so on. The list can be extended indefinitely. What writers like Moi and Fetterly want to argue, however, is that these distinctions are purely strategic: they do not refer to absolute standards of right and wrong. While there is some force in this point there is also a good deal of sophistry. If women have been oppressed by men, that is surely absolutely, not relatively, wrong – for what could it be relative to? And while their moral distinctions may not be absolute they are surely objective? It is simply a fact that women have been repressed (if that is how we see things) – and indeed, feminists claim that to be the case. This leads to a curious muddle in which the oppression of women is announced as an objective *fact* in one sentence while the possibility of objective *judgments*, historical or otherwise, is denied in the next. This muddle is the result of a confusion between different notions of objectivity: as scientific reality and as regulative principle. The first has been largely discredited, but without the second the work of Moi and Fetterly would itself be pointless. It is valuable only insofar as it has something truthful to tell us about the world, our condition and its literature. Objectivity as a regulative principle or operative ideal provides us with a methodological starting-point for critical enquiry. Assuming that we admit the possibility of telling the truth about the world in the first place (which many radical theorists do not, though they seem to admit the possibility of telling truth about theory), it is the first duty of academic life to reveal, test and transmit those truths insofar as they concern the discipline in question. It is only to that end – as Socrates pointed out – that strategic or rhetorical presentation is desirable. We know from experience that some judgments about literature are more truthful than others. We know from logic that to deny this point is to render critical discourse futile by narrowing it down to the mere articulation of textual interpretation unfettered by any context other than desire.

But desire is what radical feminists want to institute as the core of criticism. They want to deny the Kantian assertion that aesthetic judgments are characteristically interest-free, in the name of political revolution, just as liberal feminists want to deny it in the name of cultural relativism. Both see the idea of neutrality working in favour of patriarchy. And in their view, it is precisely in so-called aesthetic judgments (not to speak of the very concept of aesthetic judgment) that ideological dispositions are most clearly revealed. For this reason, art is to be seen not as apart from politics but at its very heart. The aesthetic is merely another form of the political. Criticism is therefore a form of partisan activism. For although literature does not reflect reality it does embody ideology – a curious distinction which is essential to the radical rewriting of texts.

This view has some dangerous casualties. First among them is Kolodny's insistence that academics should remain sceptical about their own assumptions. As we have seen, Kolodny is not overscrupulous herself when it comes to wild generalizations about 'female self-consciousness' and the fictionality of literary history, but she is a model of virtue compared to many radical theorists. Sandra Gilbert, for example – holder of a prestigious chair and co-author of the influential *The Madwoman in the Attic* – makes great parade of her rigour, but unblushingly announces that any possibility of feminist criticism ever being boring or trivial is something 'I am not only unwilling to discuss but constitutionally unable to consider',[14] and she seems quite pleased about it. In the same essay she expresses outrage at the fact that so few colleagues (male or female) have taken much interest in her important work. This is ingenuous, but not half so ingenuous as her grumbling about the dereliction of those who fail to attend her lectures, which she evidently considers a moral duty for students and teachers alike. They must be a frivolous lot. Certainly, Gilbert herself cannot be charged with frivolity. She seriously describes her own work as 'almost bracingly ontological' and coyly confesses to the reader that some of her best friends are men because they agree with her views. Her enemies (and they are legion) appear to be people who 'rarely go anywhere except to the faculty club and whose most common out-of-class reading is TV Guide'.[15] Perhaps they are scared away by Gilbert's crushing cultural snobbery, self-importance and ideological hustling – or is it simply that they are 'constitutionally unable to consider' the ideas Gilbert finds so ontologically bracing because they are her own?

Among the minor casualties of reducing criticism to the taking of sides is a sense of humour. This has often been remarked by commentators on radical theory, and equally often rebutted by theorists who insist either that there is no room for humour in serious debates, or that what counts as funny is determined by bourgeois chauvinists anyway. The only effective reply to such claims (short of being swept up in dismal discussions about the ideological status of humour) is to point to the dank world in which friends are politically vetted and intellectuals live in a ghetto protected from the horrors of the TV Guide. English readers familiar with the *Scrutiny* era may be tempted to ask Gilbert whether she thinks her tone – at once whining and bullying – is likely to appeal to any but the converted? Her writing is typical of the worst RLT in the contempt it shows for the very audience whose interest is vital for the currency of her ideas. There is not much point in complaining about lack of attention when one has locked the tower door on the inside.

Gilbert and her like confuse seriousness with earnestness. The point is worth emphasizing because RLT is so inclined to portentousness, and so inclined to mistake its own sense of importance for the real thing. This is itself a rich source of comedy, of course. When Julia Kristeva lectures us on the poetic power of the turd, or Luce Irigaray celebrates the babbling habits of female orifices, there is little to do but laugh. The best feminist critics, like the best male critics, are usually those with an acute sense of the potential absurdity in their own activities. But that, of course, requires a strong feeling for the relationship between theory, criticism, literature and the world of ordinary life – something RLT actively discourages, except when it is finding humour in the doings of bourgeois criticism.

Perhaps the most serious casualty of equating literature

with the workings of ideology, and criticism with ideological demystification, is any notion of literature as something which can expand our imaginative horizons, not simply confirm our ideological prejudices. This often takes the form of what we might call thesis criticism – the desire to make all the evidence, however recalcitrant, fit the writer's thesis. As such it belongs to the worst kind of academic writing, though this is frequently disguised by spurious novelty. In *The Madwoman in the Attic*, for example, Gilbert and her partner Susan Gubar are absolutely determined to make every nineteenth-century woman novelist conform to their claim, based on Harold Bloom's theory of poetic paternity, that women writers have been constantly repressed by the patriarchal myth that creativity is essentially male. As Terry Lovell – herself an excellent feminist critic – has shown, this is just plain wrong: for every instance of male creator myth in literature there is a female equivalent. But Gilbert and Gubar have to ignore this because it cuts across their identification of female creativity with subversion, disruption, absurdity, modernity and madness. In another context, Gubar even surpasses Gilbert in unintentional comedy when she remarks, à propos the same theme, that 'Margaret Anderson and Jane Heap's desire for a radically new kind of art is brilliantly illustrated by the *Little Review* volume that consisted of sixty-four blank pages'.[16] What a good example for radical theorists.

The whole topic of 'imagination' is vexed in radical theory, especially in feminism. Many feminists want to think of it, like experience, as something characteristically female: inward, tentative, intense, the natural resort of all those in flight from the so-called 'real' world dominated by patriarchal culture. But others – especially Marxists – regard imagination as a mystified and mystifying bourgeois notion, a romantic way of concealing the real roots of creativity which reach down not into some dark inner world but into that ideology which it is the radical critic's task to demystify. Others again see imagination as just another name for the demystifying process itself, in the Althusserian or Machereyan sense that literature is seen as a sort of self-critical apparatus, an auto-deconstructing machinery in which ideology is both presented and subverted at the same time.

This is the view favoured by many French feminists who want to go beyond the liberal demand for a subversive reinterpretation of literature to the claim that literature is somehow already intrinsically subversive. There are obvious similarities with deconstructive assertions (of the sort made by de Man) that it is not the critic who analyses the poem but the poem which has already analysed itself, but in deconstruction this remains a formal assertion, a description of the way things are. Radical feminists want to make it the basis of what Moi calls textual politics. She contrasts this aim with the sexual politics of liberal feminists who remain part of the bourgeois establishment by virtue of their reliance on bourgeois concepts of experience and imagination and – more importantly – their belief in the aesthetics of reference. What matters to liberal feminists is what literature portrays and how it is interpreted. Radical feminists, rejecting the idea of a distinct sphere of aesthetic experience, want to transcend it in the politics of difference. What matters about literature for them is not what it shows but what it does and how it is used.

The central issue in this new politics is the myth of patriarchy; its main instrument is a textual critique of that myth which takes us to the heart of the radical project. Patriarchy is an ideological formation embodied by radical feminists in a straw man who is white, heterosexual, Western and bourgeois. His biological gender is irrelevant, for the point about patriarchal ideology is that it shapes the attitudes of both men and women, and literature is one means of doing just that. It enforces belief in individuality, objectivity, the value of experience, bourgeois morality, the aesthetics of reflection, and all the hierarchies of man and woman, parent and child, black and white, heterosexual and homosexual, which are so offensive to radicals. It works in favour of the bourgeois, political, and social status quo which is effectively a male status quo, and it does so through every branch of political, social and cultural institutions, both directly and indirectly. Art is one of its subtlest indirect tools and the idea of neutrality or objectivity in criticism is one of its most powerful weapons. By these means it is self-reinforcing, persuading us to accept its own standards by which to judge even ourselves. In particular it is a way of persuading women to accept the 'male' valuation of themselves. In nineteenth-century fiction, for example, this works by always presenting women as inferior in status, strength, initiative and intelligence to men; or, more subtly, suggesting that when they are strong, intelligent etc. they are more like men than women.

Radical theorists believe that liberal critics are right to attack patriarchy through an analysis of its appearance in particular texts, a practice which involves charting the misrepresentation of women and their institutional wrongs; but criticize them for making the mistake of remaining caught up in what Moi calls 'depoliticizing theoretical paradigms'[17] such as the notions of experience, imagination, reference, and the aesthetic, outlined above. What is needed, in the radical view, is not an attack on the symptoms but on the cause. It is not the manifestations of patriarchy feminists should focus on, but its production of the very critical concepts we use. This is why theory must take priority over criticism.

The broad lines of the radical attack have been outlined in the last three chapters and there is no need to recapitulate them in detail here. Feminism has drawn on deconstructive approaches to textuality and Marxist approaches to ideology to mount its assault on patriarchy, at the same time criticizing practitioners of both doctrines for their own patriarchal attitudes in a complication of mutual antagonisms impossible to disentangle.[18] However, to these sources and to the structuralist account of language as a differential (not referential) system, radical feminism has added another vital element only briefly touched so far: Lacanian psychoanalysis, in particular Lacan's notion of the Unconscious.

The feminist appropriation of Lacan has not been made easier by that master's own apparent misogyny and the suspicion that the Freudian psychoanalysis which Lacan claims single-handedly to have rediscovered is patriarchal in its very nature, founded as it is on an analysis of sexuality which presents the female only in relation to the male whose penis she lacks and envies. Radical feminists have preferred to ignore this tiresome side of Freud in favour of Lacan's linguistic theory of the psyche. Lacan distinguishes two significant phases of infant psychic development: (1) the Imaginary, corresponding to the pre-conscious, pre-Oedipal life in which the child identifies with the mother and does not distinguish between itself and the world; and (2) the Symbolic, in which the child progresses (if that is the right word) to identification with the father, who stands for law, order and authority. This progression is made possible by the child's entry into language, for it is only in language that the differences necessary to a sense of self-hood and identity can be articulated.

Feminists argue from this that women are therefore relegated to a secondary role by the very medium through which they acquire their sense of identity as women. Even the order of nouns and pronouns in language (he/she, man/woman) embodies the fundamental hierarchy which structures it and which is an essential feature of bourgeois ideology, within which woman is invariably characterized as secondary, negative, other – whatever the male is not. Insofar as woman resists this order, she can be seen as subversive of patriarchy. But if we link this Lacanian account of the linguistic construction of gender with the Derridan idea of language as differentially, not referentially determined, two consequences result: (1) that language is the medium through which our sense of the world is both acquired and disrupted; and (2) that an attack on linguistic hierarchies might be made the basis for an attack on political realities.

These two principles are the basis of textual politics,[19] and they involve a complicated alliance between contemporary theories of psychoanalysis, deconstruction, Marxism and feminism. Putting the matter at its crudest, the feminist version of RLT finds political equivalences between women, the unconscious, the proletariat, and literary interpretation. All are repressed by bourgeois ideology in the interests of a patriarchal political order. The freeing of one is therefore closely related to the liberation of the others. RLT's role is to contribute to this general liberation through its attack on bourgeois hermeneutics.

✱ We can see one approach to this in the earlier work of Julia Kristeva, who has now swung surprisingly far to the political right, but in her salad days based theories of sexual, political and critical revolution on a variant of Lacan. Kristeva claimed that while patriarchal ideology works in literary texts to conceal unwelcome truths, these truths can nevertheless occasionally be observed forcing their way through to the surface, rather as unwelcome aspects of the psyche, however fiercely confined to the unconscious, force their way through to consciousness, albeit in indirect form. The fiercer the repression, the more explosive the outcome; so it is in modernist texts, which represent the collapse of bourgeois ideology, that we see the conflict at its bitterest, revealed in cracks and fissures, contradictions and dislocations – though Kristeva suggests that these are always at work to some degree in poetic language which is, by nature, subversive. 'Literature' is thus defined as that which is subversive of its own rules, because it establishes complex conventions only and always to undermine them to a greater or lesser degree. The same is true of that greatest achievement of bourgeois society, the concept of the individual subject, which is similarly breaking down under the pressure of its own internal contradictions.

Now whatever the merits or demerits of this as an historical or psychological scheme, it is no better than Kolodny's relativism when it comes to providing a new basis for critical pedagogy. Kolodny reduces criticism to a sort of glorified subjectivity which amounts to belle-lettrism with sociopolitical pretensions. She fiddles with the syllabus but does nothing about the curriculum. This is simply bourgeois academic criticism in a new guise. Kristeva, more drastically but with equal futility, turns criticism into an ideological trial in which the text's right to silence is construed as an admission of guilt: what it doesn't say in those cracks and fissures gives the game away. But this is also to reduce criticism to the interpretation of meaning, turning the literary academy into a thimble-hunt, perpetually on the lookout for something whose identity is already known. There is some educational value in that, I suppose – on a par with asking questions about multiplication tables – but not much. Nor does it provide grounds for condemning bourgeois critics, when radical theorists, too, are simply looking for confirmation of their prejudices.

Radical theorists are rightly scandalized when bourgeois critics lazily invoke reality as their criterion of literary value without further comment. But what is the point, if the only consequence is to substitute 'ideology' for 'reality', with the disadvantage of added complications? When Toril Moi rebukes her Anglo-American colleagues for the weaknesses in their theory of ideology, pointing out that if it were as effectively despotic as they claim, they would have no way of knowing that fact, she doesn't propose to sweep away the theory as so much useless lumber. Instead, she refines it, suggesting a definition of ideology which accommodates contradictions whose increasing inner conflicts eventually force us to become aware of them. This is no remedy at all, since it leaves the concept of ideology where it always was: in the land of hypotheses where Freud's 'unconscious' and Marx's 'economy' rub shoulders with the theologies of

Augustine and Origen, or almost any Western philosophy one cares to name. In each case, an enabling fiction in the form of a metaphysical principle is postulated in order to make the system work. But as in the cases of Christian theology and Western philosophy, the fictions become more and more complex and qualified until they are worse than useless. Ideology is just another enabling fiction or metaphysical principle of this sort. Increasing refinement deprives it of dramatic force without strengthening credibility. It is already joining the queue reserved for heaven and hell, absolute spirit and the rest.

More to the point, these fictions are taken to exemplify the very objective judgments radical feminists refuse to believe in. The existence of ideology becomes a fact. The claim that there are no value-free judgments – itself a value-free judgment – is taken as axiomatic. The radical feminist project to subvert all values becomes contradictory when subversion is assumed to be a positive value without further comment. Most ironic of all, the liberal academy which looms so large in feminist demonology – that creation of *soi-disant* male chauvinists – turns out to be the very stage on which they parade their claims. The idea that the academy might be a neutral sphere of discourse is simply opposed with the assertion that there is no neutral sphere – that everything, in the famous phrase, is political: as though it were not because of that, not in spite of it, that we need to cultivate disinterestedness somewhere. The fact that there are always interests at stake and in conflict in every human activity is not a radical discovery but one of the commonplaces of classical liberalism, which radicals invariably conflate with positivist ideals of scientific objectivity. It was, of course, the very philosopher who characterized the aesthetic as the realm of disinterested judgment – Kant – who described the world as a place of permanent and necessary conflict. But one could hardly expect radical feminists to bother with such a point. They are too busy dismantling the straw man of patriarchy.

7

Readers and Writers

'That is the supreme pancake,' he said. 'If
you could say what the shouts mean it might
be the makings of an answer.'

In the last four chapters I have tried to show that RLT, far
from being the engine of dynamic political change in society
at large, cannot even introduce reform into the literary
academy. Its improvements on conventional critical practice
turn out to be just that – a continuation of bourgeois criticism
by other means; or a move to dispense with the study of
literature altogether, except as an adjunct of the other human
sciences. Despite minor changes in the syllabus and some
fiddling with the curriculum, it offers no way forward, just
more of the same, or complete abolition. Radical theorists
end up squabbling over terminology or lapsing into tame
pleas for the introduction of Discourse Studies, which turn
out to be rhetoric in a new hat. Ritzy talk about ideology,
subjectivity, textuality etc. adds icing to a well-known cake,
but does nothing to solve the institutional problems of literary
pedagogy. The burning question for academics is: how are
they going to put their own house in order before someone
else does it for them? The literary academy has no divine
right to existence, and its role in Western education, though
still enormous, has begun to shrink. Internal doubts about its
function, fuelled by RLT, are now being intensified by
internal and external pressures.

These pressures are enormous. Although theory's challenge
inside the academy has been largely naturalized, thereby
losing most of its force, it has been around just long enough

and with sufficient strength to demoralize traditionalists – without opening the way to anything new. The situation is exacerbated by the disappearance of 'English' (and French, German etc.) as a natural unity. Where there was once an evident tradition and a homogeneous body of undergraduates, there is now vast cultural and ethnic diversity. We can no longer assume knowledge of the Bible, Shakespeare and British history among our pupils. An education which evolved to cater for the small company of upper- and middle-class Englishmen with a common outlook, is now expected to accommodate all races, classes and attitudes. When taken together with severe financial retrenchment and an attempt (largely resisted within the academy) to find ways of making the humanities vocationally relevant, these social changes make the traditional syllabus look increasingly irrelevant.

The conventional literary academy has responded to these pressures by tinkering with the syllabus, but has not modified its basic assumption, which is that literary education is valuable primarily by virtue of its moral and cultural content. The encounter with great literature is salutary of itself: the ways in which we manage this encounter are neither here nor there. The student is taught how to make fine moral and psychological discriminations, how to become self-aware, how to recognize human relationships and predicaments in the texts he studies; and in the process he is expected to acquire a working knowledge of English (or French, Italian, German etc.) culture and history, whose relationship to the syllabus is unproblematic. This approach has begun to look a little threadbare in recent years, not because these ends are deplorable (though RLT would claim that they are misconceived) but because they hardly add up to a coherent, self-conscious educational programme in a complex society where there is little agreement about what constitutes history, culture and morality; and because such an approach, with its assumption that literature relates directly to life, sits so uneasily with other disciplines in higher education. What equivalence could there be between such a notion of literature and, say, chemistry or geology, which are founded as disciplines not on moral grounds but on elaborate procedures, technical vocabularies, and practical applications in the world outside the academy? Even literature's sister subjects, philosophy and history, have more claim to disciplinary respectability than she does in these respects.

In recent years, humanist teachers have learnt to support their literary studies with a more positive approach to diverse cultural sources: the syllabus has been broadened to include black literature, women's literature, etc. etc., and these now sit side by side with Shakespeare. But the result has been more confusion than ever, since there is no agreement about the criteria according to which such revisions are made. Shakespeare remains in the syllabus because he has always been there, and people feel uneasily that, as a mainstay of our culture, he must be. Women's literature is there either because it is demanded by an interest group, or because someone feels guilty. In neither case are clear reasons for the presence of either topic given. On the contrary, most time is now taken up in English departments arguing why this rather than that should be on the syllabus and in what context. Do we teach Shakespeare on his own? As a Jacobean dramatist among others? As part of a great tradition? As one writer among many? As an option? As part of courses in tragedy, comedy, etc.? In the literary context, the cultural context, or the political context? As an Englishman, a European, or a Westerner? The choices are endless.

Radical theorists are inclined to deal with these problems by theorizing them, which boils down to replacing Shakespeare's texts with critical arguments about them as the topic for study. This has its virtues, but it isn't a solution to the problem, which is merely pushed back a stage. Instead of arguing about how to teach Shakespeare, we argue about the selection of critical theories. This may be a pedagogic improvement, or it may not, but it alters only the context (and the difficulty) of the syllabus, not its nature. We stay where we were.

One advance on tinkering with the syllabus is tinkering with the curriculum,[1] and this has proved popular with radical theorists who like to teach literature in a new context, putting English, for example, together with other vernacular literatures, or even with history and philosophy. This is little more than a revival of the old Cambridge Tripos, but it has merits, not least the advantage of encouraging students to look at the concept of 'Literature' with a more critical eye. Putting literary texts next to philosophical texts, for example, brings out strategic and rhetorical features often neglected – not to speak of the epistemological, ontological and metaphysical features which so exercise radical theorists. But the practice raises more problems than it solves – that is its value. It still doesn't give us a reason for studying literature rather than chemistry, or even provide any basis for supposing that it can provide the foundation for a coherent academic discipline. On the contrary, putting literature next to philosophy (or history) is to raise all sorts of doubts about the status of both – doubts recently explored by theorists ad nauseam.

In short, it seems that literary studies, which only a brief time ago looked set to dominate the revived human sciences, are about to undergo the fate of philosophy and theology, which once played the same role: gradual attrition leading to marginalization. It may well be that this fate is unavoidable and even desirable. There is no special merit in size, and a reduction in scope might have the salutary effect of making teachers of literature think more carefully about the purpose of what they do, instead of leaning on conventional practice to carry them through, or flying off into the never-never land of theory. A more likely outcome is that English will lose its disciplinary independence and turn to servicing more worthwhile activities, such as Business Studies and Hotel Management. Literature teachers will abandon cultural legislation in favour of polishing prose for day-release students in colleges of technology.

Needless to say, that is a doom regarded with unqualified horror in university and polytechnic departments, which is a pity. Those who have tried it know that it might do us all a great deal of good, simply by forcing us to confront literature at its most basic level: as writing. This is a shock to the system for the average Higher Education teacher – especially the average radical theorist – who inveterately thinks of his work in terms of reading. Take one look at the theories discussed in this book. For most of them it is axiomatic that even the writer is really a reader. Even Marxist attempts to construct a theory of literature as a mode of production emphasize the reader's role in producing the meaning of the text, not the author's role in writing it. 'Author' is a dirty word in radical circles, where the hermeneutic drive is so strong that every theory is itself the subject of instant rereading. In consequence, critical pedagogy has been narrowed down to the interpretation of meaning, literary training to the acquisition of interpretive paradigms. We are reminded over and over again that texts are constructed, but radical theory is largely indifferent to the skills and techniques which go into constructing them, so intent is it on rhetorical and ideological analysis. Theorists seem to forget that writing is a practical activity, even as they bang on about criticism as a 'practice'. An obsession with semantics obscures the fact that, for the writer, words and sentences, paragraphs and chapters, tropes and punctuation, are all instruments in the service of a larger project. So violent is resistance to the notion of literature as communication that most radical theorists cannot entertain for a moment the idea that a poet or novelist may be doing what they themselves do: looking for effective ways of transmitting their thoughts. A few weeks teaching electronic engineers how to describe their summer holidays would soon cure that.

There is, happily, an alternative to teaching literature either

174

in this basic form, or as a debased adjunct to history and philosophy – a way which might even combine the advantages (there are some) of both, besides doing something better. That is to teach it as music and art are taught in vocational colleges and departments, where the emphasis is on learning conventional practices in performance, and the acquisition of relevant technical skills. In literary terms, this means matching the teaching of reading with the teaching of writing.

This, too, will no doubt be regarded with horror in respectable literature departments in this country, where 'writing' as an academic discipline is deprecatingly – and legitimately – associated with the dismal Composition, Journalism and Creative Writing courses of minor American universities. The problems with these courses are well known: their tendency to reduce writing either to the mechanics of rhetoric or the pathos of self-expression; the consequent encouragement they give to think of writing either as a sequence of technical tricks or as substitute psychotherapy; and their complete detachment from critical skills the student may or may not be acquiring in more conventional courses. These problems are compounded by the ludicrous 'modular' pattern in American education (sadly infecting the British system) whereby students can elect to do completely unrelated courses which they must then somehow cobble together into a coherent degree scheme. But of course, just as there is little practical use in learning to read unless one learns to write at the same time, the reverse is also true. Experience with small children also suggests that the two skills are closely linked, and that they reinforce one another. The only worthwhile way of teaching literature in the sense I am suggesting, therefore, is in a highly integrated, closely monitored structure. Once again the parallels with music and art are apt. In musical training, critical and theoretical work is only useful when closely allied to practical studies. Learning to write one's own music (however primitive) is an essential part of learning to read and perform the music of others.

I am not suggesting that a vocational approach to literary studies should replace what we already have – any more than I would advocate closing down musicology and history of art degrees in university departments. But I am proposing a change of emphasis. What this means in terms of a theory of literary pedagogy is a shift in attention from interpretation to composition, from values to skills, from the preoccupation with meaning to the study of conventions. The two terms in each pair cannot be separated, but they can be given different priorities. In critical theory, for example, we can learn to make our first question 'How does the text work?' not 'What does it mean?' This still leaves infinite scope for every kind of interpretation, from the most scrupulous scholarly and historical reconstruction to the rereading of recent theorists, but it puts both of them in context as literary practices, not as political therapies. What would interest the student of literature as a writer is technique before meaning, even when looking at classic texts. How Dostoyevsky, for example, manages his brilliant ensemble scenes; what Proust does with syntax; Eliot's manipulation of symbolism; Chaucer's deployment of the iambic line; and so on. Radical semiology makes elaborate gestures towards such a practice, but invariably lapses into the crudest and most banal kind of ideological analysis, which is simply devoted to discovering in the text in question what we want to find, in ways not worthy the name of an academic discipline. Far more important and relevant to the student of literature are questions of medium, genre, technique, convention and skill.

No doubt it will be said that such an approach does nothing to remedy the questions posed by theory, and nor it does. But it can make them look a good deal less urgent. Once we expand our approach from hermeneutics to include other skills, we no longer need to agonize over the problems of foundationalism unless we choose to. Musical studies do not require ultimate metaphysical and epistemological grounds: these are a matter for the individual student. What the academy gives him or her is a body of conventionally validated practices in performance, composition, etc. – practices which are governed by the immediate realities of solving problems. Even in musical studies, of course, one can be a Marxist or a Platonist or a Pythagorean; but in the end you must play your cello or compose your symphony as well as you can, and your teacher is there to help you do that, not to cast doubt on the very grounds of your being.

In short, it is time we realized that the study of literature depends upon learning skills: it is not a degenerate human science, but an art. It does not belong in Aristotle's misleading trinity of poetry, philosophy and history, but with music and painting. As such it has cultural and social value of its own, quite apart from any political significance attaching to this or that school of criticism. This is the answer to those on the right who would like to reduce literature teaching to grammar and syntax; to those on the left who want to make it the engine of political change through radical theory; and all the others, right, left and centre, who think that literary studies are an extension of ideological indoctrination in any cause, however good or bad.

There is nothing new in such an approach, of course. On the contrary, what I am suggesting is a return to the past, to the traditions of a truly humanist literary curriculum as prescribed by theorists from Aristotle to Ramus – a curriculum in which what Renaissance writers called analysis and genesis, and what I am calling criticism and composition, or reading and writing, are reunited to form a coherent pedagogic whole wherein the disinterested pursuit of excellence can once again take its legitimate place. Only then will the literary academy rediscover its sense of purpose and a role in the world.

NOTES

1. The Problem

1. In *Critical Practice*.
2. Reprinted in *Writing and Difference*, pp. 278–95.

2. Mythologies

1. *Textual Power*, p. 43.
2. They draw very different conclusions from it.

3. The Science of Literature

1. *Roland Barthes by Roland Barthes*.
2. *Criticism and Truth*.
3. Quoted in P. Rieff, *Freud: the Mind of the Moralist*, Chicago University Press 1979, p. 204.
4. R. Jakobson, *Questions de poétique*, p. 603. Cited in J. Culler, *Structuralist Poetics*, p. 56.
5. In *A Prague School Reader*, ed. P. Garvin, Georgetown University Press 1964, p. 23.
6. D. Sperber, 'Claude Lévi-Strauss' in *Structuralism and Since*, ed. J. Sturrock, p. 28.
7. From *The Savage Mind*, quoted in Sperber, op. cit., p. 22.
8. In *Sémantique structurale*, pp. 45–7.
9. *A Reader's Guide to Contemporary Literary Theory*, pp. 59–60.
10. See *Introduction to Poetics*, chapter 1.
11. In *Figures of Literary Discourse*, chapter 7.

4. The Bliss of Ignorance

1. *Allegories of Reading*, p. 119. See also p. 19 for the title of this chapter.
2. Ibid., p. 57.
3. R. Pattison, 'Trollope among the Textuaries' in *Reconstructing Literature*, ed. L. Lerner.
4. *Blindness and Insight*, p. 87.
5. *Allegories of Reading*, p. 3.
6. *Blindness and Insight*, p. 10.
7. *Allegories of Reading*, p. 10.

8. Hartman's *Criticism in the Wilderness*.
9. De Man has already valued these writers by choosing them. If they constitute an alternative canon, it is precisely the canon standing behind the tradition of phenomenological criticism to which de Man owes so much.
10. From *Swann's Way*. De Man uses his own translation. The passage can be found in Kilmartin's translation of *A la recherche du temps perdu* (Chatto 1981), vol. 1, p. 89.
11. *Allegories of Reading*, p. 14.
12. *Interpretation, Deconstruction and Ideology*, pp. 68 ff.
13. *Allegories of Reading*, p. 57.
14. In *Beautiful Theories*.
15. *Writing and Difference*, p. 272.
16. See note 10 above.
17. *Allegories of Reading*, p. 18.
18. Ibid., p. 17.
19. Idem.
20. *Blindness and Insight*, p. 127.
21. *Allegories of Reading*, p. 285.
22. Ibid., p. 286.
23. *The Critical Difference*, p. 5.
24. *Deconstruction: Theory and Practice*, p. 106.
25. The phrase recalls de Man's claim that he has used 'only the linguistic elements provided by the text itself . . .', *Allegories of Reading*, p. 17.
26. *Deconstruction: Theory and Practice*, p. 106.
27. *Literary Meaning*, p. 199.
28. Idem.
29. *Allegories of Reading*, p. 270.
30. In *Writing and Reading Differently*, ed. Atkins and Johnson, p. 140.
31. Idem.
32. *The Critical Difference*, p. 7.
33. *Writing and Reading Differently*, p. 140.
34. *Blindness and Insight*, p. 18.
35. *Writing and Reading Differently*, p. 140.

5. Memories and Reflections

1. *Metahistory*, p. 283.
2. *Studies in European Realism*.
3. *The German Ideology*, Lawrence and Wishart 1963, p. 39.
4. W. Dowling, *Jameson, Althusser, Marx*, p. 83.
5. T. Eagleton, *Marxism and Literary Criticism*, p. 18.

Notes

6. *The German Ideology*, p. 2.
7. In *Criticism and Ideology*, p. 142.
8. *The Political Unconscious*, p. 35.
9. Ibid., p. 225.

6. Girls on Top

1. In 'Toward a Feminist Poetics', *The New Feminist Criticism*, ed. E. Showalter, pp. 125–43.
2. 'Dancing Through the Minefield' in *The New Feminist Criticism*, pp. 144–67.
3. Ibid., p. 148.
4. Ibid., p. 151.
5. Ibid., p. 153.
6. Ibid., p. 154.
7. Ibid., p. 160.
8. Ibid., p. 160.
9. Ibid., p. 156.
10. *Sexual/Textual Politics*, p. 71.
11. 'Dancing', p. 163.
12. *Sexual/Textual Politics*, p. 71.
13. *The Resisting Reader*, p. viii.
14. 'What Do Feminist Critics Want?' in *The New Feminist Criticism*, op. cit., p. 41.
15. Idem.
16. 'The Blank Page and the Issue of Female Creativity' in *The New Feminist Criticism*, p. 308.
17. *Sexual/Textual Politics*, p. 76.
18. But see K. A. Reader's *Intellectuals and the Left in France since 1968*.
19. *Sexual/Textual Politics*, pp. 150–67.

7. Readers and Writers

1. For what it is worth, my own model for a new curriculum would look something like this:

   (1) Rhetoric and criticism – the detailed study of texts.
   (2) Composition – the production of texts, to be closely linked with course (1).
   (3) History – lectures on literary forms and genres, relevant cultural and political contexts etc.
   (4) Critical theory and literary theory.

Notes

The first two courses would be taught in small seminars or individual tutorials, the second two by lecture. Needless to say, there is enormous scope here for squabbles about what history, theory etc. should be included, but there seems to be enough scope in three years to cover aspects of just about everything. (3) and (4) would anyway be subordinate to (1) and (2).

BIBLIOGRAPHY

Althusser, L. *For Marx*, Verso 1979
Atkins, M. and Johnson, G. (eds.) *Writing and Reading Differently*, Kansas University Press 1985
Barthes, R. *Writing Degree Zero*, Cape 1967
— *Mythologies*, Cape 1972
— *Critical Essays*, Northwestern University Press 1972
— *S/Z*, Cape 1975
— *The Pleasure of the Text*, Cape 1976
— *Roland Barthes by Roland Barthes*, Macmillan 1977
— *Image-Music-Text*, Fontana 1977
— *Criticism and Truth*, Athlone 1987
Belsey, C. *Critical Practice*, Methuen 1980
Booth, W. *The Rhetoric of Fiction*, Chicago University Press 1961
Bruss, E. *Beautiful Theories*, Johns Hopkins University Press 1982
Butler, C. *Interpretation, Deconstruction and Ideology*, Oxford University Press 1984
Culler, J. *Structuralist Poetics*, Routledge and Kegan Paul 1975
— *The Pursuit of Signs*, Routledge and Kegan Paul 1981
— *On Deconstruction*, Cornell University Press 1982
— *Barthes*, Fontana 1983
De Man, P. *Blindness and Insight*, Oxford University Press 1971
— *Allegories of Reading*, Yale University Press 1979
Derrida, J. *Speech and Phenomena*, Northwestern University Press 1973
— *Of Grammatology*, Johns Hopkins University Press 1976
— *Writing and Difference*, Routledge and Kegan Paul 1978
Dowling, W. *Jameson, Althusser, Marx*, Methuen 1984
Eagleton, T. *Criticism and Ideology*, Verso 1976
— *Marxism and Literary Criticism*, Methuen 1976
— *Literary Theory*, Blackwell 1983
— *The Function of Criticism*, Verso 1984
Empson, W. *Seven Types of Ambiguity*, Pelican 1972
Felperin, J. *Beyond Deconstruction*, Clarendon Press 1985
Fetterly, J. *The Resisting Reader*, Indiana University Press 1978

Bibliography

Frye, N. *The Anatomy of Criticism*, Atheneum 1957

Genette, G. *Figures of Literary Discourse*, Oxford University Press 1982

Gilbert, S. and Gubar, S. *The Madwoman in the Attic*, Yale University Press 1979

Graff, G. *Literature Against Itself*, Chicago University Press 1979

Greimas, A. J. *Sémantique structurale*, Larousse 1966

Harland, R. *Superstructuralism*, Methuen 1987

Hartman, G. *Beyond Formalism*, Yale University Press 1970

— (ed.) *Deconstruction and Criticism*, Routledge and Kegan Paul 1979

— *Criticism in the Wilderness*, Yale University Press 1980

Hawkes, T. *Structuralism and Semiotics*, Methuen 1977

Irigaray, L. *Speculum de l'autre femme*, Minuit 1974

Jakobson, R. *Selected Writings* (4 vols.), Mouton 1962

— *Questions de poétique*, Seuil 1973

Jameson, F. *The Prison-House of Language*, Princeton University Press 1972

— *The Political Unconscious*, Cornell University Press 1981

Jefferson, A. and Robey, D. (eds.) *Modern Literary Theory*, Batsford 1982

Johnson, B. *The Critical Difference*, Johns Hopkins University Press 1980

Kristeva, J. *Desire in Language*, Oxford University Press 1980

Lacan, J. *Four Fundamental Concepts of Psychoanalysis*, Penguin 1979

Lerner, L. (ed.) *Reconstructing Literature*, Blackwell 1983

Lévi-Strauss, C. *The Savage Mind*, Weidenfeld 1966

— *Structural Anthropology*, Allen Lane 1968

Lukács, G. *Studies in European Realism*, Merlin 1972

Macherey, P. *A Theory of Literary Production*, Routledge and Kegan Paul 1978

Merquior, J. *Foucault*, Fontana 1985

Mitchell, W. (ed.) *The Politics of Interpretation*, Chicago University Press 1983

— *Against Theory*, Chicago University Press 1985

Moi, T. *Sexual/Textual Politics*, Methuen 1985

Montefiore, A. *Philosophy in France Today*, Cambridge University Press 1983

Mulhearn, F. *The Moment of Scrutiny*, Verso 1981

Norris, C. *Deconstruction: Theory and Practice*, Methuen 1982

Bibliography

— *The Contest of Faculties*, Methuen 1985

— *Derrida*, Fontana 1987

Picard, R., *Nouvelle critique ou nouvelle imposture?*, Paris 1965

Propp, V. *The Morphology of the Folk Tale*, University of Indiana Press 1958

Ray, W. *Literary Meaning*, Blackwell 1984

Reader, K. A. *Intellectuals and the Left in France since 1968*, Macmillan 1987

Rorty, R. *Philosophy and the Mirror of Nature*, Blackwell 1980

— *The Consequences of Pragmatism*, Harvester 1982

Scholes, R. *Textual Power*, Yale University Press 1985

Selden, R. *Criticism and Objectivity*, Allen and Unwin 1984

— *A Reader's Guide to Contemporary Literary Theory*, Harvester 1985

Showalter, E. (ed.) *A Literature of Their Own*, Princeton University Press 1977

— *The New Feminist Criticism*, Virago 1986

Sturrock, J. (ed.) *Structuralism and Since*, Oxford University Press 1979

Tallis, R. *Not Saussure*, Macmillan 1988

Todorov, *Introduction to Poetics*, Harvester 1981

White, H. *Metahistory*, Johns Hopkins University Press 1973

Widdowson, P. *Re-Reading English*, Methuen 1982

Williams, R. *Marxism and Literature*, Oxford University Press 1977

INDEX

Index

Fontana Press

Fontana Press is the imprint under which Fontana paperbacks of special interest to students are published. Below is a selection of titles.

- ☐ A Century of the Scottish People, 1830–1950
  T. C. Smout £6.95
- ☐ The Sociology of School and Education *Ivan Reid* £4.95
- ☐ Renaissance Essays *Hugh Trevor-Roper* £5.95
- ☐ Law's Empire *Ronald Dworkin* £6.95
- ☐ The Structures of Everyday Life *Fernand Braudel* £9.95
- ☐ The Wheels of Commerce *Fernand Braudel* £9.95
- ☐ The Perspective of the World *Fernand Braudel* £9.95
- ☐ France 1789–1815: Revolution and Counterrevolution
  D. M. G. Sutherland £5.95
- ☐ Crown and Nobility, 1272–1461 *Anthony Tuck* £4.95
- ☐ Racial Conflict in Contemporary Society
  John Stone £3.50
- ☐ Foucault *J. G. Merquior* £3.50

You can buy Fontana Press books at your local bookshop or newsagent. Or you can order them from Fontana Paperbacks, Cash Sales Department, Box 29, Douglas, Isle of Man. Please send a cheque, postal or money order (not currency) worth the purchase price plus 22p per book (maximum postal charge is £3.00 for orders within the UK).

NAME (Block letters) _____

ADDRESS _____

_____

_____